Spy Rules

By Lew Serviss

ISBN-13:
978-1463695927

ISBN-10:
1463695926

For Naomi, my muse

This is a work of fiction. Any resemblance to actual persons, living or dead, events or locales is entirely coincidental.

Front cover photograph by Jake Rome
Back cover photograph by Ben Serviss
Design by John de Dios

Spy Rules

Prologue

They crept out of the jungle.

North, the thin American, had brought night-vision binoculars, but the full moon provided enough light to stay on the trail. The airfield ahead had enough candle power for a Super Bowl; the illumination drew clouds of hideous insects from the swollen Orinoco River. Here the mighty river formed the muddy border of Colombia and Venezuela.

The band advanced: Twenty Colombians; a dozen Yanomamo tribesmen; North and three beefy Americans; two guides – Pablo and Bolivar – from nearby Puerto Ayacucho. As they drew closer, their quarry came into view – 20 gleaming Russian jet fighters, Sukhoi Su-30MK2s. These were Mach 2 additions to the Venezuelan Air Force, with a range of about 2,000 miles – the distance from Caracas to Washington. They could reach the Lincoln Memorial in under two hours.

The band carried 400 pounds of C-4 explosive, more than enough to reduce the jets to $1 billion worth of dust.

The group slipped around the perimeter of the air base toward its soft spot, far from where a company of Venezuelan infantry was garrisoned. Intelligence suggested security was lax because of the notion that the base's remote location made it inaccessible to attackers. It was the same bit of logic that the Soviets had employed: Put a fence around the country, but not the nuclear arsenal itself.

In early October, the rainy season was reluctantly drawing to a close, and the trail was slick with mud. Anacondas were the chief concern in the wet river basin. Bolivar suddenly dropped to the muck as the tall grass ahead rustled. A caravan of a dozen capybara – four-foot-long rodents that resembled St. Bernard-size guinea pigs – scuttled across the trail in the direction of the river. North marveled at how all the creatures of the South American jungle were oversized and extra deadly. He had been horrified by a giant Caranguejeira – a spider that looked like a hairy Alaskan king crab – that had crawled up the wall of his thatched hut in the Yanomamo village upriver where they had prepared for the attack.

They continued on, fingers on their Kalashnikovs. Bolivar stopped at their destination: a length of wire fence well in the shadows of the base lights. One of the Colombians came forward to begin to cut a hole.

Snip.

The sound was largely masked by the cacophony of chirps, whistles and shrieks of the wild.

Snip.

Suddenly, floodlights. The Americans instantly dropped and rolled into the high grass. The rest stood squinting into the light – deer mesmerized by high beams. The Americans began to crawl quickly, keeping low, feeling the whoosh of high volume, large-caliber fire. They heard the thud of bullets finding flesh. The rest of the team was cut down in seconds without a chance to cry out in anguish.

They had been waiting.

Chapter 1

Ross Walton shuffled up Eighth Avenue and around the corner at 44th Street. He slowly descended the dirty steps into the Times Square subway station. An October chill took the edge off the stench of urine. He frowned at the winking bearded man in the poster for a cheap vodka and turned right into the tunnel under the tracks where during lonely hours a brisk trade in rape, robbery and homicide flourished. He flashed his NYPD shield and the cashier in the bulletproof booth gave a sideways look at the trim, white-haired old man, then a look of comprehension, and he remotely unlocked the entrance gate.

Underneath the glue-on wrinkles and eyebrows and water-based hair color, Ross was a wiry 32-year-old decoy cop. He was the worm dangled to subway predators. Technically, he was required to get into costume, and character, in the transit detectives substation in Times Square station. But within a department of 36,000 cops policing seven million inhabitants, a lot of the regulations were only winked at. Technically, Ross' banishment to transit detective was a promotion for a job well done. Ross and everyone else in blue knew better.

Ross entered the windowless squad room, a gloomy subterranean collection of battered institutional desks and ignored paperwork. Coffee cups abounded, but no one ate down here; subway rats were not to be trifled with.

"No one person has had more of an impact on this country," said Joe Gaughan, a thickly built member of Ross' three-person backup team.

"No way. Let me think about this for a minute," said Ginny Quinn, the senior member of the subway team. She frowned as Ross walked in and turned away before their eyes met. "Sirhan Sirhan? No way."

The third member of the crew, Jose Calderon, noticed Ross. "It's supercop," he said, not in a friendly way. Gaughan glared, then returned to his treatise. "Think about it," Gaughan went on, "without Sirhan Shirhan, Bobby Kennedy becomes president. No Nixon, no Watergate. No Ford, no Jimmy Fuckin' Carter. Who knows what the country would be like today." The three subway cops contemplated what if. Ross broke the silence. "Let's fucking go already."

After hours of riding packed rush-hour trains, studying the clumps of commuters stripped of their personal space, they had arrested an ass-grabbing teen-ager, a pelvis-grinding businessman and a belligerent door holder (with an outstanding arrest warrant for a month-old stabbing). As the crowds thinned later in the evening, the crew moved to a Brooklyn-bound R train in search of bigger game.

Ross, wizened and muggable in his disguise, sat in a car toward the back of the train. His natural hair color was brown; women found his eyes soulful and his angular face rakishly handsome. At an inch below six foot, but a slender 170 pounds, Ross easily transformed into tempting prey. Gaughan and Quinn, in an adjacent car, watched him through the connecting door. Calderon did the same from the car on the opposite door.

Ross, like most subway commuters, kept his head down and studied shoes. In two years as a decoy, he had drawn some strong correlations between shoe style and predatory behavior. Five feet to his left was a pair of scuffed black laced shoes, Hispanic male, 40s, most likely an office worker; five feet to his right, high-top Chuck Taylor sneakers, white female, 20s, probably an NYU student; across, work boots, caked with mud, husky black male, 30s, construction worker.

Chuck Taylors got off at Pacific Street and was replaced by steel-toed work boots, black male, 20s – trouble. He chose to sit two feet to the right of Ross, who glanced to see if Calderon had noticed. (He couldn't tell.)

Muddy work boots got off at Ninth Street and scuffed black laces at 25th Street. The car was getting lonely, but steel-toed boots slid next to Ross: Step 1 from the subway muggers' handbook.

"Whattup, old man?" A gold tooth rounded out the menace as he smiled. He was close enough for Ross to smell nicotine. Ross looked for Gaughan and Quinn but saw no faces through the train door. He nodded, a slow, stiff old man nod and waited for the move. The young man formed a fist as he launched a right hook targeted for the center of Ross' face. Ross leaned away from the punch, which landed on the graffiti-resistant Plexiglas window behind him. Ross grabbed a fistful of hooded sweatshirt with his left and raked the attacker's face with his right elbow. He flung the mugger to the floor, climbed on top and leaned into four short punches that caught the right side of his face. Ross pulled his compact Beretta from the holster in the small of his back.

"Whattup? You're under arrest, shitbag. That's whattup," he said, nudging the back of the mugger's head with the pistol. Ross looked left and right for signs of his backups storming in from the adjacent cars. Nothing.

The mugger groaned. Ross cuffed him tighter than was necessary. He took a .25-cal. pistol from the mugger's left pocket and a gravity knife from his right. He pulled his prisoner to his wobbly feet and waited for the train to pull into 36th Street.

On the platform, he met up with his three backups. "I'll take him," Quinn offered.

"The fuck you will," Ross replied. "You douche bags enjoy the show?" Stoned-faced, the three followed Ross and the prisoner up the stairs and out to the street, where they summoned a squad car. Passers-by stared at the old man holding the young handcuffed man by the forearm.

******

Ross walked into Flynn's still in old-man disguise. He slid onto a stool beside Laura.

"Oooh, the old-man suit makes me so hot," she said.

"Yeah, it makes the bad guys lose control, too." Ross surveyed the Tuesday night scene. The bar was thinning out at 1 a.m. Half of the drinkers were four-day-a-week Alphabet City locals; the rest were tourists or junior Wall Street titans on a New York nightlife safari.

Albert appeared from around the corner of the horseshoe bar. He shook hands with Ross. "How ya doing, grampa? That's a good look for you. Rock? Cabo?"

"Yes, Albert, and a needle to inject it." Ross couldn't understand half of what Albert said with his lilting Irish accent, but the barman always enunciated when it came to drinks. Ross' beverage preferences rarely shifted.

"Rough night?" Laura asked. She worked as a jewelry designer and spent most nights holding court at the bar. She and her boyfriend, Sam, who was usually locked away in perpetual crunch time for a video game his company was working on, lived down the block. Flynn's was the living room for many fledgling Lower East Siders with precious few square feet of dwelling to call their own.

"Ah, usual shit," Ross said. Albert shuffled down behind the bar to join their conversation. Ross saluted with his tequila shot, downed it and took a long slug from his beer. "I'm just gonna eradicate that memory from my brain."

"That's the way," said Albert. "I'm only staying in the States till me liver gives out."

Ross and Laura looked at each other and laughed. "Where does he come up with this shit?" Laura said.

Ross guzzled his beer and tried to forget the festering stench of the subway. Albert replaced a drink for each hand, loudly slapping the bottle on the bar with mock fury. Ross raised the shot glass and called out to the barroom: "To Albert's liver!" The regulars cheered; the rest looked confused and annoyed at the drunken white-haired geezer. The crowd picked up as people arrived alone, in pairs and in small groups. Rudy, the bodybuilding bouncer, created a line out the door as he carefully checked everyone's ID.

"How's Candy?" Laura asked.

Ross frowned and shook his head. "Gone."

Laura put her glass down before it got to her lips. "Huh? What?"

"I threw her out."

"Wow. Want to talk about it?"

"Not much to say. She was a skanky coke fiend and I kicked her out." He took a pull of his beer. "I should have had her arrested."

"What did she do?"

"She forged a check for $500 to buy coke. Thought I wouldn't notice." His jaw clenched. "That's what she told me, 'I thought you wouldn't notice.'"

"Wow. I am so sorry." She rubbed his shoulder.

"Look, it's no big deal. I should have done it long ago. Move on, you know? Have lots of mindless sex."

"Albert!" she yelled across the bar. "This man needs another shot!"

Albert appeared with three shot glasses filled with blue liquid.

"What the hell is this?" asked Ross.

"Old family recipe," Albert said. "Leprechaun

juice." The three of them clinked glasses.

"To mindless sex," offered Laura.

"My favorite," said Ross.

"Is there any other kind?" said Albert.

Laura and Ross walked to the back to play the arcade game Moose Hunt. Though Ross was drinking furiously, his marksmanship was extraordinary. He beat Laura three games in a row.

"Damn it!" she said. "Do you know how much I practice this stupid game just to beat your ass?" she said.

"A waste of valuable drinking time," he said.

They walked back toward their spot at the bar. Laura squeezed past a group constricting traffic. Ross stopped at the bottleneck.

"Hey, excuse me, pal," Ross said, not politely, to a burly man wearing a leather vest over a black T-shirt. The vest could have been motorcycle gang colors, but it wasn't. Another poseur, Ross thought.

"What the fuck's your problem?" the vest said. He looked quizzically at Ross. The unflinching brown eyes didn't seem to fit the rest of the picture. Ross took a step toward him, but Rudy had been tracking the encounter and was there to head him off.

"Come on, Ross. Not tonight, man," he said softly. He turned to the vest. "It's OK. I got him. Don't worry about it." The vest could not have been happier to have the scary giant brown man on top of the situation.

Rudy put his arm around Ross and walked him back to Laura. Half the bar watched.

"Do me a favor, hit someone tomorrow night," Rudy requested. "Anton's working the door."

"Yeah, yeah," Ross said. "Hope that Vagisil's working out for you, Rudy."

Rudy shook his head. "Why are you such a fucking ball buster? When do I get good cop? It's always bad cop."

"You know I got your back. Don't you?" Ross said.

"Yeah, yeah."

"Who took the piece off that kid last month?"

"You did, Ross. You just can't give the customers a beat down. It's bad for business."

"Yeah, I'm an asshole," Ross said. "I admit it."

"Yes," Rudy said, "You, my friend, are an asshole."

Ross sat down with Laura, but glared toward the vest and his group. They looked warily at the crazy old man, or whatever he was. A minute later they filed out. The last one in line, a girl with long auburn hair, looked back at the crazy codger. Ross grabbed her ass. She scooted out of the bar without a second glance.

"Man," said Laura. "You are in a state tonight." Ross shrugged. "Why do you like to fight so much?"

"I don't know." He gulped his beer. "It's something to do."

"You are weird."

"That's a nice way of putting it."

Albert came by and mumbled something that neither of them understood.

"Is it that we're drunk, or is he fucking with us?" Laura asked.

"Both."

"Hey," Laura pointed with her chin. "Tattooed lady at 10 o'clock." Ross downed his shot of Cabo Wabo reposado and chased it with a long slug of Rolling Rock. He was feeling the glow. More importantly, the images of his surly backup team and the gold-toothed mugger were melting from his head. They were becoming a blue goop, like Albert's Leprechaun juice.

"I think I know her," he said. "Beth, or Nancy or something. Works in the leather shop on Avenue A."

"Leslie."

"Right, Leslie. I wasn't even close, was I?" He laughed hysterically. "She got drunk off her ass the night we all played poker. Fell off her stool. Thought she broke her arm." He studied her across the bar. An angry Slayer song played on the juke box, and Ross signaled for another round. Albert set down the shot and beer. He saw where Ross was looking and stage-whispered, "I think she's a guy."

"Shut up, Albert."

He carried his beverages to the other side of the bar and sat down.

"It's Leslie, right?" She was tall and lanky, with raven hair that set off what little pale skin that wasn't covered in ink. Chinese writing covered each arm from elbow to just below the shoulder. The spaghetti strap to her tank top bisected a winged creature whose head was somewhere out of sight. Ross wondered about her private gallery. She stared at the spry old man before her.

"Oh wait," Leslie said, "you're that cop. Right?"

"Yep, the cop." She stared intently. He considered whether it was a dragon emerging from her cleavage. He drained the Cabo and she bought shots for the two of them.

"Are you packing right now?" she asked quietly, leaning close to be heard and speaking slowly so that her boozy tongue would function properly.

"Armed and *very, very* dangerous," he said. Leslie giggled, Her laughter built until her eyes teared and she laid her head in her arms on the bar.

"What?" Ross asked.

"You look like" – more hysterical laughter – "Dick Van Dyke. But not Rob Petrie Dick Van Dyke. Present-day Dick Van Dyke."

"And you look like Mary Tyler Moore. But not Laura Petrie Mary Tyler Moore. Mary Tyler Moore with a shitload of tats." Ross looked across at Laura, who gave him a thumbs up. "Do you own any Capri pants?" he asked Leslie. She pointed a finger at her temple, as if to facilitate thinking, and scrunched her eyes.

"I don't know," she said. "Why don't we go check?"

She lived, like most young residents struggling to

pay exorbitant rents in the formerly crime-infested Alphabet City, in a studio apartment the size of a cage at the zoo. Ross wanted to rinse out the white-hair dye and lose the wrinkles, but she insisted she wanted Dick Van Dyke. And she did indeed find a pair of Capri pants and put them on, if only briefly. He beheld the swirl of color, her dragons, eagles, setting suns and moons, the whole exhibition that lay before him.

"OK, here's our theme," she said. "This is the night – before we moved into the house in New Rochelle – when we made Richie."

"Oh that's good. That's very good. I can definitely work with that."

"But first," she said, "you have to tell me what you did tonight. Did you lock anyone up?"

He told her about the mugger and how his backup team had ignored the take-down.

"But I don't get it," she said. "That doesn't make any sense."

"Not supposed to. It's the po-*leez* department." Her confusion gradually lifted.

"Oh. Like Chinatown."

"Forget it, Jake." Ross touched his nose to hers. "You really want to do this?"

"Hell yeah. I always wanted to fuck a badass cop."

"Doesn't everyone. Hey, is that Noah's Ark on your back?"

Chapter 2

The Americans made it to the tree line seconds before a helicopter took off sweeping a light around the perimeter of the base. Five of the Colombians and two Yanomamo had also survived. The guides were gone, so North led the band toward the river. Every five minutes he halted and took 360 surveillance with the night vision binoculars. There seemed to be no pursuit.

Even so, when they found the dugout canoes that had brought them across the wide river they waited for the next patrol boat to pass by. Only then did they shove off, paddling hard against the strong current. They were all dappled with the blood of the ones who had been shot. North longed to rinse off in the river, but he wondered how many piranha swam in the brown water beneath them. They were done if the helicopter found them in the open water, but there was nothing in the air.

They bumped land on the Colombian side and scurried ashore. Ten minutes farther west, they stopped. North retrieved a satellite phone from his pack.

"This is the garage," said a voice on the other end.

"This is Pinto. I need a tow truck."

"When?"

"Yesterday would be good."

"What's the problem?"

"Two flat tires on Highway 61."

"Roger that."

They hacked through thick jungle on a northwestern heading, bushwacking toward a trail that would make the rest of the evacuation a simple matter of one boot after another. Flocks of bats buzzed them. The jungle had a pungent aroma: dampness, decay, the beginning and ending of life. A gang of squirrel monkeys followed them in the trees, shrieking taunts. The humid air hung like a spray.

As they paused for water and a moment's rest, North replayed the abrupt turn of events: They had left the village, paddled downriver, slipped through the jungle to the wire – and were cut to ribbons. This was the part that he knew would be unpleasant.

When he got back to Miami he'd have a Cuban sandwich and a mojito. His mind always drifted to food when he was in the middle of the bush, minus any of the creature comforts. Years ago, camping in Big Bend, he and his high school friends had spent days listing all the things they'd eat once they got back to Houston.

They marched on. Walking the trail in daylight would be dangerous, and he wanted to cover as much ground as they could in the dark.

******

"Hey, sleepy head." Leslie nudged Ross awake. "Do you have to be somewhere? Catch robbers or something?" She was dressed and looking fresh, even though they had been thoroughly drunk and hard at work when the first gray light appeared.

Ross had a familiar headache. Did he drink too much? Or not enough? "What time is it?" He remembered sighting the Eiffel Tower, but couldn't place where. Someplace not visible on the clothed Leslie. He had been amazed to find that Leslie, otherwise a walking gallery of art, lacked a tattoo in the small of her back.

"It's eleven. I guess you work nights?" She waited

as he struggled to open his eyes. "Want some coffee?"

"Um, no. Got a beer?"

"Oh, you are just so ready to die." She retrieved a Corona. His head hurt and his throat burned from smoking too much. He took a swig and lit a cigarette.

"I know this doesn't look good," he said. He got out of bed and put on his pants.

"Not so much. No," said Leslie. She giggled. "You still have the … " She pointed to his hair, still colored white.

"Oh Jesus. Can I use your shower?"

"Sure." She bit her lip.

"What?"

"You're a nice guy."

"This comes as news?"

"Well, it's not what you project."

"I'm self-destructive, I admit." He held up the beer. "Self-medicated."

She shook her head. "In bed, you were," she searched for the proper words, "kind of sad."

Ross stared wide-eyed. "*Now* I'm pained."

"No, no. I don't mean the sex wasn't good. Just that you seemed," she darted her eyes left and right in search of the proper description, "off somewhere. In a sad place. I'm sorry." She shook her head at herself. "I'm not explaining this right at all. Look, I have to get going. Stay as long as you want. Don't get me wrong, I'd like to do it again. Maybe as you and me, not Rob and Laura." She kissed him. "Make the city safe, OK?"

The shower, built to the same proportions as the apartment, seemed designed for someone without elbows. Ross stayed under the steaming water much longer than it took to rinse the old man out of his hair.

Leslie was right: He *was* a sad soul. The truth was that Ross had begged Candy to stay after he discovered the forged check. She was the only constant in his life other than a dangerous job surrounded by colleagues who wanted to put a bullet in his face. Candy, who ingested more cocaine than food, had called him pathetic and slammed the door, leaving him alone with a life strewn with regrets.

****

They made it to the trail with an hour to spare before daylight. It began to rain a fine mist that the Americans found soothing; they were traveling quickly and perspiring heavily. Dried blood made it appear as if they were wearing copper sun block.

The jungle heat was building. The Colombians and Yanomamo were indifferent to the conditions. They wanted only to steer clear of the leftist rebels who operated in this eastern fringe of Colombia and deliver the Americans. The job had paid well, and they had survived.

They stopped to catch their breath and drink the last of their water. North checked the GPS and found that they were close – very close.

They pushed on behind North as the black sky turned gray and the jungle noise grew louder and more varied. Howler monkeys began an ear-splitting call and response. The men rounded a bend and came upon a band of guerrillas not ten feet away. Amid the cacophony, the rebels hadn't noticed the interlopers. They carefully retreated, but not before the Americans took stock: Sixteen rebels with rifles. Beyond them lay the airstrip.

North checked his watch: They had 20 minutes at the most. One of the stocky men spoke to him, shouting in his ear to be heard over the monkeys. North nodded, and the two of them passed on the plan. The stocky man put his pack down and got to work. After two minutes he signaled a thumbs up.

The five Colombians ran back around the bend and fired bursts at the guerrillas, dropping five or six of them. The rest of the rebels charged into the jungle after the attackers. The Colombians ran back to the rest of the band, waiting deep in the jungle off the trail. As the rebels drew near, the stocky man tapped a small box and detonated two bricks of C-4 he had placed in the middle of the trail. The blast triggered a devastating wave of expanding gases that simply erased whatever was in its path. There was no need to fire at survivors; there was no trace of the dozen rebels.

The explosion silenced the monkeys. The band walked past the crater that marked the blast site and around the bend past the bodies.

The airstrip was merely a wide clearing of grass and eroded earth in the jungle, not even fit to be a fairway on an under-funded public golf course. It rose steeply to the east. At the downhill end lay a thick tangle of towering trees.

They heard the plane. The Americans nervously scanned the perimeter as the Cessna 206 banked sharply around the trees and touched down. It stopped at the high end of the strip and pivoted to face downhill. The others smiled broadly when the Americans dismissed them with handshakes and waves.

"Leave your shit!" the pilot yelled over the prop when they opened the door. "Wicked crosswind. It's gonna be hairy, son. This strip is full of holes."

North saved his satellite phone and night binoculars. The others dropped their packs and scrambled on board. The pilot motioned North into the copilot's seat and handed him a headset. He revved the engine and started down the field, toward the trees, barely going fast enough for the slow lane of the freeway.

The Cessna bounced over the rutted surface as the wind shoved it left. North determined the true reason for dumping their extra weight: the pungent green scent of bailed plant matter piled in the rear. Why else would an American come to this part of the world to attempt suicide maneuvers? North wondered if any outsiders came to South America pure of heart.

"Wish I'd ordered the turbo engine," the pilot

said. His accent sounded southern, perhaps Arkansas. Mirrored sunglasses completed the stereotype. "Aw, fuck it. The price was right." The American adjusted his headset.

"Good thing we're not too high up," North said. "With the heat and humidity, we'd be fucked."

"We may be fucked anyway." The plane shuddered as a wheel took the full brunt of an enormous crater. "Here goes nothin'." The wheels left the ground, but barely, the pilot keeping the big Cessna in ground effect, riding the cushion of air to gain speed. The trees grew larger each second.

"C'mon, baby," the pilot coaxed. His expression was one of amusement. North remembered that in many corners of the world, giggling was a natural response to the fear of death.

After attaining more speed, the pilot pitched the nose up and the plane slowly climbed, its belly pointed at the cluster of trees. The Americans looked at one another, wide-eyed.

"Let's show 'em, darlin'," the pilot said. He banked the plane sharply left in front of the trees. "Fuck, yeah! That is some fun shit right there. Ain't that a kick in the ass?"

The monkeys resumed howling.

Chapter 3

Lyle Rucker strode to the lectern as the audience rose and applauded. Rucker waved. He found his 27-year-old wife, a former Dallas Cowboys cheerleader, in the first row and pointed. He imagined a band playing and thousands of balloons being released as he stood waiting to deliver his acceptance speech as his party's nominee for president of the United States.

"Ladies and gentlemen, it is my great pleasure to be here today to dedicate the Lyle J. Rucker Wing of Houston Baptist Hospital." More applause. The people sitting in the rear, 150 employees of Rucker's company, Aero Exploration, rose but instantly sat back down when Rucker motioned to them.

"I'm just a Texas boy from a little border town called Laredo." Wild applause. "So I am truly blessed to be able to stand here today and help dedicate this wonderful medical facility that will be able to help so many, many people in need. It just underscores that with the help of the Good Lord, any American can find success if they're willing to work hard.

"On behalf of my beautiful wife Debbie over here – " he pointed at the first row, and as Debbie stood to exhibit her curves, the 150 Aero employees, bused in from company headquarters, whooped and hollered.

Rucker smiled and started again. "On behalf of Debbie and myself, I want to thank the board of Houston Baptist, the hospital administrator, Dr. George Barson, and most of all, the Rev. John Stanton Nesmith, who had the vision and the inspiration to ask me for the money to make this possible." Gales of laughter. "Just kidding, Reverend. Ladies and gentlemen, thank you very, very much, and may God bless."

As Rucker handshaked his way down the dais, he stopped to whisper in Reverend Nesmith's ear. "Reverend, if you've got another idea how I can put up $10 million and make $40 million, you have my number." The reverend laughed heartily and squeezed Rucker's shoulder.

Rucker liked being a philanthropist. After growing up in need, to be able to help so many people was a dream come true. He'd build an entire hospital, for children with cancer, when Aero planted its flag in Maracaibo. He'd build a ball field for the kids in his old neighborhood in Laredo. He'd buy Debbie another sports car. She deserved it for putting up with his Viagra-driven libido. He was 59, but silver-haired and trim – because of her. No one mistook her for his daughter; clearly he was a powerful business titan with a trophy wife of the first magnitude.

Hell, why would he need to be president?

"I'm off to Neiman Marcus, sugar," Debbie said once they were outside the hospital auditorium.

"I'm sure they've missed you," Rucker joked.

Debbie smiled vaguely. "The benefit next week? I have got to find something appropriate to wear."

"Anything you wear is appropriate, darlin'." Debbie gave him a peck on the cheek and walked off. Rucker caught up to his aide, Matt North.

"Matt, ride with me," Rucker said. "We need to talk about that thing down south."

In the limo, Rucker poured himself a Scotch and contemplated the passing streets. North sat opposite him, nursing a bottle of spring water. He and Rucker could have been father and son. North was tall and lean, perhaps an inch shorter than his six-foot-two boss. Slender, but broad shouldered with a strong chest – a study in lean muscle. His hair was thick and black. His face was at once rugged – with prominent cheekbones – and boyish – a delicate nose. It was a combination that made most women melt.

"I never get tired of this town, Matt. It's a far cry from scratching in the dirt in Laredo. This is the land of opportunity, but you have to grab it. Take the initiative."

"Yes sir, you do."

"When did you get back?"

"Got into Miami the day before last."

"Feeling OK?"

"Nothing worse than a sunburn, sir."

Rucker's expression hardened, though his tone remained even. "Matt, just what in the hell happened down there?"

"We were set up, sir. The Colombians helped us organize the mission, but turned around and told the Venezuelans. They were sitting there waiting for us."

Rucker drained his glass, looked out the window and crossed his arms. "Cocksuckers," he said softly. North gave him a detailed chronology of the operation, ending with the daredevil rescue by the crazed bush pilot hauling Colombian weed.

"That just tears it," Rucker said. "I thought they had their honor and such. Just a bunch of thieving cut-throats." His face reddened as he thought of the South American gangsters chuckling at such an easy mark. Suckers. Rubes.

North said nothing. They drove on in silence.

"Is the New York operation still functioning?" Rucker asked finally.

"Yes sir. Everyone's been quite happy with it." Rucker swept his hair with his hand and studied the office towers of downtown Houston. "But of course, now it's an affront to us," North said.

Rucker studied the lunchtime crowd of coatless businessmen and comely, well-dressed women. A steakhouse would be nice, he thought. His own place where he could entertain small parties for intimate dinners. A Houston version of the "21" Club – hell, Nixon used to keep his cigars waiting for him there. "It's good to have goals," his daddy had told him, though he'd never accomplished a single one of them.

"Son, not much on God's green earth goes in a straight line," Rucker told North. "I certainly never thought I'd be sitting in my own skyscraper in downtown Houston when I started out in business steam-cleaning carpets. One thing leads to another and along the way you learn some things.

"That's right, sir."

"I think this enterprise of ours needs to start a new chapter. Show them that if they cross us, we can shut that well down. You get my drift?"

Matt North, recruited off the campus of Baylor by the Central Intelligence Agency eight years earlier, knew exactly what needed to be done.

******

The car pulled in front of the mammoth red-granite U.S. Embassy and the Ambassador slid into the back seat, followed by his military attaché. They pulled away from the 27-acre mountainside campus overlooking Caracas and were joined by a Venezuelan military escort. The motorcade cut through the chaotic traffic of Caracas, moving west to the Casa Amarilla, home of the Venezuelan Foreign Ministry.

"So what did we do this time?" the ambassador asked. "I'm sure we're being summoned to be accused of something imperialistic."

"I wish I knew," said the attaché. "But it's OK. I spent two and a half years in Syria. I'm used to it." They both chuckled.

The motorcade wound down Avenida Bolivar to the Plaza Bolivar and pulled into the grounds of the Casa

Amarilla, the yellow colonial building built on the grounds of an old prison.

They were escorted into the office of Foreign Minister Jorge Montador, who did not invite them to sit. Montador glared at them individually.

"I will make this brief," he began. "Your country has committed an act of outrageous aggression against the Bolivarian Republic of Venezuela. A commando squad launched an attack on the Air Force base at Puerto Ayacucho. Our soldiers killed most of this renegade band, but some of them escaped. We demand that they be returned to face justice."

"Where is your proof, sir?" the Ambassador demanded.

The Foreign Minister ignored him. "We are considering expelling you, and recalling our ambassador from Washington over this offensive act of imperialism. Until that decision is made, we will require you to confine your travels to Caracas. Good day, sir."

Dismissed, they returned to their car for the trip back to the Embassy.

"Yep," the attaché said, "just like in Syria."

******

Ross sat in the last car of a Brooklyn-bound L train. He needed no disguise for the day; he came as himself – hungover, sleep-deprived, unshaven, dull-witted. Protocol called for him to ride in a car somewhere in the middle of the train so that his backups could observe. But that system was clearly rooted more in nostalgia than safety. The shoes on this train were poor: scuffed and mud-caked. Some wore flip-flops, the most desperate of shoes, even as autumn took hold in New York. Ross shut his eyes and drifted off to sleep.

He dreamed of his father. Shoulder-length sandy hair. Closely cropped beard. Blue eyes. The sort of free spirit from a small upstate town who would meet the love

of his life at the Woodstock festival. That would be Ross'
mother. She was a tough chick from the Lower East Side
with raven hair and piercing brown eyes. Sicilian on both
sides. Doug had eaten five tabs of acid and Linda had
smoked several bowls of hash. During the first few acts of
the first day, the blitzed crowd stared at the trees and the
grass and one another while the music washed over them.
Doug and Linda noticed each other in the massive
undulating crowd during Ravi Shankar's set and
gravitated together. Doug's aura was light blue and warm
to the touch, she would say.

He would follow her home to New York, where
her father would chase him away, screaming in Italian
and waving a .38. They ran away together to his
hometown upstate. They lived in an old clapboard house
with a leaky roof that fronted the main road through town.
He repaired motorcycles and they ate as much trout as he
could catch in the Delaware River. Eight years later,
along came Ross, named for Roscoe, N.Y., his birthplace.

In the dream, Ross and his dad were fishing on a
charter boat in the ocean. The sun was shining, the breeze
was blowing. Ross was sure he would catch the biggest
fish he'd ever landed.

"I think I got one, Dad," he said, as he felt a gentle
tug on his line. His father smiled. "I'm gonna get a big
one, Dad." His line snapped taut. "Dad?"

His father smiled again, in that gentle way, but
said nothing. And then Ross got a sickening feeling as he
remembered: Dad was dead, stabbed by a junkie after
they'd moved back to New York. Doug Walton was never
cut out for the city.

Ross was alone, holding a fishing rod. His line
was slack; the fish was gone.

He woke up as the train jerked and pulled away
from the First Avenue station. The car was empty except
for an unshaven white man sitting across from him. The
man sprang at Ross and put a hunting knife to his throat.

"Give me your wallet, or I'll cut your fucking

throat wide open," he said in a hoarse whisper.

Ross stared into his eyes. The man's pupils were the size of dimes.

"Do it," Ross said softly. "I don't fucking care." The robber tightened his grip on Ross' jacket. His teeth were stained and chipped. He smelled of screw-top wine.

"Come on, come on," the man snarled.

"Kill me," Ross urged. "Come on. If you're a killer, prove it."

The man gritted his teeth and reached for Ross' pocket with his knifeless hand. Ross flashed to his father, knifed in the back on Rivington Street in a crime as senseless as this one. A war cry shot out of Ross' throat as he grabbed the wrist of the knife hand, drove the top of his head into the mugger's nose and rode the man to the floor of the subway car. He buried his shoulder into the man's collarbone as they hit the floor. The robber shrieked in pain.

The backups burst into the car.

"What did you do to this man?" Ginny Quinn demanded of Ross.

Chapter 4

Ron Margolis got his mouth around a three-inch-thick pastrami on rye and took a hungry man bite.

"For my money," chew, chew, chew, "this is the best deli in New York. Better than the Carnegie."

Yehuda Shapiro didn't seem to hear him. He stroked his beard and stared out the window. Pedestrians whizzed by on 47th Street. Most of them were talking on cell phones. Traffic was at a standstill, and agitated drivers were playing the soundtrack of Midtown Manhattan on their horns.

"I remember when these guys were out on Queens Boulevard," Margolis said. Shapiro rearranged his skullcap, gave another tug on his beard and put both hands flat on the table. He couldn't understand how Ronnie could be so carefree – and hungry.

"Ronnie, tell your people I can't do it."

"What?" Margolis swallowed a wad of pastrami. "Yehuda, this isn't exactly a request. These people don't fuck around."

"I don't understand," Shapiro said. "Why do they want us to stop? Our southern friends are happy. I'm happy. The way it's going, I can match what I'm making from the shop. This is a gold mine, pardon the expression. I'd be *meshugga* to stop now."

Margolis sighed. His tongue searched for stray

pastrami particles.

"The rule with dealing with these people is not to ask too many questions," Margolis said. "To know the answers is to get yourself killed."

"Killed," Shapiro repeated. "They'd kill you? Kill a police detective?"

"Like brushing their teeth in the morning. I told you when we set this up, if you go in, it's completely by their rules. We have no leverage in this. I'm taking my guy's money and you're getting a nice split from the …" he looked around and lowered his voice to a whisper, "the Colombians." The waiter approached and Shapiro asked for the check.

"We've known each other, what?" Margolis asked.

"Since we were little *pishers* sitting on the stoop in Williamsburg," Shapiro answered. "Long enough." Margolis fingered the Glock on his belt.

"Look, here's what I'm going to do. I'll tell my guy we talked."

"We *did* talk."

"We talked and you said OK. You'll shut it down with our amigos." Outside, a Hasid walked down the street and Margolis wondered how many thousands of dollars worth of uncut diamonds he had folded up in a cloth in his pocket. "Then, whatever you do, you do. Just, be smart about this, *bubbala.*"

Feeling as if his tongue sandwich had gone down sideways, Shapiro left the restaurant and blended into the stream of bearded men with black fedoras and long black coats.

It didn't make any sense. He hadn't wanted to get involved with the Colombians in the first place, but Ronnie had pushed and pushed. Shapiro had to admit, the Colombians were very professional. No complaints. And now they were supposed to act as if nothing had happened. As if all the money that was flooding in didn't matter. Well, it did matter.

Shapiro crossed Sixth Avenue to the Diamond District. His father had passed the store, Shapiro & Sons, to him, and he would pass it to his son soon enough. He walked inside and the girl at the counter told him that Manny and Hector were waiting in the back.

"Oy," he said. Hustling to his office, he locked the door behind him and greeted the Colombians. They removed a bill counter from the closet and began to feed it stacks of hundreds. In five minutes, the machine counted out $560,000. They loaded the cash into Shapiro's safe.

"Manny?" Shapiro began.

"Yes?" Manny said, meeting his eyes. Shapiro wondered how many corpses Manny had looked at as routinely as he now looked at the jeweler.

"Any problem with the gold?"

"Oh no. It all goes right through, and then we melt it. Just like a magic trick. I hope our children will continue this fine business, Senor Shapiro." He squeezed Shapiro on the arm and smiled with his mouth, but not with his dark eyes.

"Well then, this is for you," Shapiro said. He shook aside a sheet covering three large boxes. The Colombians looked inside to find solid-gold belt buckles, wrenches, ladles and butter knives.

"Bueno," Manny said. "Muy bueno."

******

Dennis Bouton leaned back in the deck chair and let the breeze wash over him. The sun felt luxurious. The scent of hyacinth and the squeals of gulls affirmed that he was far from the Beltway. He opened his eyes and savored the turquoise water of Biscayne Bay.

"Freshen your drink?" asked Rafael, framed by a pair of wind-swept palm trees.

Bouton stirred from his trance. "Oh. No, I'm great." He gestured with his drink at the tropical panorama. "This is breathtaking, Raf. I always love coming here."

"I think this is paradise," he said. "I had the chance to buy Nixon's place, but … " He swept his arm toward the horizon in explanation that this was the superior view in Key Biscayne.

"To get back to your question, Dennis, you want Mirtle and his group for this operation. They are top notch."

"His man Vinson – he knows his stuff?"

Rafael tracked a yacht heading around the point toward Bimini, or perhaps the Bahamas. "Oh yes, Vinson has contacts and experience. He kept everything greased for one of the oil companies down there – not an easy thing to do. Those guys are very, very valuable. You're getting them at a great price."

"Good. Then that's that." Bouton stood beside Rafael and they both studied the yacht.

"He'd better turn east or he'll run aground," Rafael said. As if on cue, the yacht veered.

"What a life," Bouton said. The salt air made him want to divert to Miami Beach for stone crabs. But he needed to get quickly to New York.

Rafael thumped him on the arm. "You should move down!" he said. "A patriot like you, you could write your own ticket. I've been to Washington." He shook his head side to side in disapproval.

"Maybe one day, Raf." Bouton recalled what he knew about how Nixon had come to live in the "Winter White House." The story involved far less than six degrees of separation from the mob. No, his parents had drilled him when he was young: Don't get yourself into anything you can't explain to Jesus.

"Well, at least bring Mary down for a long weekend," said Raf. "I'm away a lot and I'd just as soon have a friend enjoy the place than leave it empty. I'm serious."

"I appreciate it, Raf." Bouton looked north,

toward the skyline of Miami.

"We've got a lot of work to do," Bouton told Rafael. "The country's depending on it."

"Don't forget," Rafael said, tapping a finger on the younger man's chest, "I am always here to help. I love this fucking country." Rafael was 16 when he floated to Key West on a homemade raft after the Bay of Pigs. Now he lived in a $24 million house.

"You've helped, Raf. And you can help some more by keeping this conversation — "

"A secret."

"Yes, a secret."

"In our world, men who can't keep a secret don't live long."

Bouton smiled and nodded as he absorbed enough of the sparkling view to hold him, at least for a short while, in Washington. His office in the Old Executive Office Building, where he spent most of his waking moments, looked out onto an airshaft. Mary loved the sea, but she also could never live with what it would take to get there.

Raf put his arm around Bouton's shoulder. "Not to chase you, buddy, but there are some gentlemen arriving here soon that you probably would never want to acknowledge meeting."

******

Ross walked to the counter of Rizzo's. "Slice and a Snapple," he told the counterman. Sammy wasn't hard to spot in the three-table pizzeria. Rizzo's still had an ancient coal-fired oven. The pizzas had a thin crisp crust and sauce that tasted like it was made by Italians.

Ross had known Sammy Napolitano since they were tough kids trying to grow up in a Lower East Side housing project. Kevlar was fashionable back then in Alphabet City, awash in heroin and crack and automatic weapons fire. Ross did what many kids of no means but with a talent for violence did: He became a cop. Not a few of his childhood friends went on to lucrative careers in organized crime.

Sammy was one of the more successful ones.

"Ros-coe!" Sammy said. "Anyone tell you lately you look like shit?"

"No, but thanks for the heads up, Sam."

"How's the Irish army?"

"They got Italian cops. I'm half Sicilian, don't forget."

"Eat your pizza, half-a-fuckin'-Italian. Someone wants to see you."

"Bacciagaloop?"

Sammy imitated a deep growling voice. "Get that fuckin' Ross kid. I gotta see 'em."

"Shit, what did I do?" Ross asked. Bacciagaloop was 73, five-foot-two, about 250 pounds and bald, a horrible dresser who wore vintage black-rimmed glasses and always had a cigar in his mouth. He was a soldier from the 1950s, holding on to the traditional ways the mob made lots of money. He could have been a capo, but he didn't want to be a bureaucrat; he cared only about running his own rackets. He ran his fief in Lower Manhattan with the goal of keeping his businesses going until he died in bed. Bacciagaloop was not someone you wanted to be asking about you.

They walked around the corner to Elizabeth Street.

"I don't think it's anything bad," Sammy said. "He didn't tell me to bring piano wire. The guy gave your mom a pledge, remember?"

"Yeah, the pledge. Lucky me."

Sammy playfully punched Ross on the shoulder and shadow-boxed. "How's the redhead," he asked. What's her name?"

"Candy." Ross made a sour expression. "Bacciagaloop should fuck her in the ass."

Sammy stopped walking. "Oh! Now that's an

image I don't want in my head. Hold it –
Redheadswithfatoldguys.com. Nah, no one's that
twisted." Among Sammy's more successful enterprises
were several porn sites.

They stopped in front of an unmarked storefront
next to a Chinese grocery.

Bacciagaloop was sitting at a small table facing
the door. He waved them in as he talked on a cell phone.

"I want the money. No debate here. Like the man
says, 'Money fucking talks and bullshit fucking walks.'
I'm not gonna tell youse again." In the opposite corner of
the small room was a large man. Sally Beans attempted to
read the sports section of *The Daily News* in the dim light.
Ross guessed Sally was six-foot-seven and about 375
pounds. He had been Bacciagaloop's driver and enforcer
for 25 years.

"Hey kid, how ya doin?" Bacciagaloop asked
Ross. The voice made Ross' throat hurt. He realized he
wasn't sure how to address the powerful Mafioso.

"I'm fine, ah, Mr. Mastroianni."

"Come on, kid. Call me Bacciagaloop. Don't
break my balls, kid."

Ross smiled. He was at an utter loss as to how to
behave. He was a New York City police detective, and
yet, he was also a kid from the neighborhood at an
audience with the top wiseguy on the Lower East Side.

"When you gonna give up that police department
shit?" He looked at Sally and they both shared a very
funny joke. Ross stood awkwardly.

"Siddown, kid. Here." He pulled out a chair.
Sammy also sat at the little table. A thin, gray-haired man
appeared with espresso for everyone.

"Look, Ross. I don't want nothin'. I made your
mother a pledge, when your dad – well. Your mother's
family been in the neighborhood a long time. We care for
our own – that's all. So how you doin', kid?"

Ross looked at Sammy. "Me? I'm great. Yeah, no
worries."

"That's good, kid. Good to see ya. Stop around if you need anything, I'm serious."

"OK."

"I'm fucking serious." He certainly looked serious.

"OK," Ross repeated. "Thanks."

Outside, Ross turned to Sammy and shrugged. "What the hell was that?" he asked.

"The old man just wants you to remember he's around. In a way, he's the police, too. He's still in charge of the neighborhood. If things get too goofy, it costs money."

"Is the neighborhood getting goofy?"

"No, it's getting Chinese. But we can do business with them, too. In fact, I've been playing hide the mortadella with the chick who runs the grocery next door. *Marrone*! Not for nothin', but you should check out these Chinese broads, if you're turning out the redhead."

"I did go out with a Chinese girl for a while. She climbed a rope at a club on the West Side."

"What the fuck is that – 'she climbed a rope'?"

"She was a performance artist. You go into this club and there's music and bars everywhere and, like, acts. Diane climbed a rope and just hung out. Sometimes she'd pose, or swing around, or climb up or down. Lots of time she just perched in the rope. Looped it around and made a seat for herself. It was fucking weird. Paid pretty good, though. "

"Fuck that. How was she in the sack?"

"She was strong, you know? She climbed a rope! Weird person – notice we're not together – but a great fuck."

Sammy extracted two cigarettes and handed Ross one. "Can I get her phone number?"

Chapter 5

At 6:30 in the morning, the mayor of New York sat in the police commissioner's conference room at 1 Police Plaza eating toast and scrambled eggs. He talked about the Rangers' chances this season with the commissioner, to his left, and the director of the Office of Emergency Management, on his other side, until the members of the anti-terrorism task force were through with breakfast and sipping coffee.

"Gentlemen," Mayor Fernando Silva began, "I have an extremely busy day today, so I won't keep you long. I have to be at a town hall meeting in Red Hook in two hours about that incinerator business and trust me, I will not be a very popular guy." The city officials, who clustered at the east end of the giant conference table, chuckled in sympathy.

"I've got a few words here, we'll go around the table and then we'll adjourn." His chief of staff handed him a binder and the mayor emptied his coffee cup as he reviewed his notes.

"I want to keep this group small. You'll notice the FBI is not here. I get regular briefings from Special Agent in Charge Owens, and I'm assured that if he were here he would play it very close to the vest. And in a second, it will be abundantly clear why he is not a part of this group. So we'll save the commissioner some eggs and coffee. I also considered having the commissioners of health and environmental protection join the group, but decided that they should work through Jim and OEM. In the case of a terrorist strike, or better yet, in the event we have some time to act on a credible threat, this group will come together.

"Naturally, protecting the city from a militarized attack is the No. 1 concern of all of us here. We've spent enough time analyzing 9/11 to know how to watch for danger and how to mobilize quickly. We've got to continue to train our people how to anticipate and how to react. We must continue to drill them on the chain of command. And we have to be continually upgrading our communications technology.

"What I want to stress today – Commissioner Steele and I spoke about this last week – is the threat from organizations – foreign and domestic – that are not targeting New York, but are carrying out murderous operations here and putting New Yorkers in harm's way. Commissioner?"

"Mr. Mayor, Bill Herron briefed me, so if you don't mind," the commissioner said. The mayor nodded.

William Herron, deputy commissioner for intelligence of the NYPD, couldn't recall a mayor as youthful and self-assured as this one. After decades of frumpy, balding, nasal old men, Fernando Silva was as dashing and charismatic as John Lindsay. Silva had worked his way up to a high-ranking position in the Manhattan District Attorney's Office, was appointed Corporation Counsel – the city's top lawyer – and in his first political campaign, walked to victory in the mayoral election. From what Herron had seen of him in action, Mayor Silva was a fast study and knew the value of a quick decision.

"Gentlemen," Herron began, "the NYPD is confident that we've built a perimeter defense against terrorist organizations that want to strike civilian-rich targets. We've got our people in all the appropriate listening posts and we continue to build on that matrix. We've got more informants in more places than ever before. Now we're organizing a second front.

"Going back probably to when the Dutch ran it, this city has presented a special kind of battlefield for governments and political interests around the world. Commissioner Steele found an NYPD study from the 1950s that found 72 foreign nations had intelligence agents operating in New York. We're in the process of a new count and I believe the number in New York today will be twice that. Just last year, we conducted a census of political refugees here and found 2,560. Of these, 61 had been cabinet level officials or higher in their countries. We consider all of these people to be targets." The mayor stopped him.

"I've instructed the NYPD to study how to contain these groups – the possibility of attacks of retribution, assassinations – so that we don't have buildings falling down when some criminal regime decides it doesn't like that its exiled finance minister is talking to *The Times*," the mayor said. "Furthermore – and this doesn't leave the room – I won't have American spooks whacking people in this city. It's our city, and they're our rules. So if they need to leave buildings smoking to further some global goal, let 'em do it in Philadelphia."

******

Shapiro made the rounds of his children.

"Good night, Papa." Yehuda kissed 5-year-old Shana and pulled the covers tightly around her.

"Good night, little *punim*."

In his four-bedroom rowhouse in south Williamsburg he housed nine children between the ages of 5 and 19. Three-level bunk beds in three rooms. Shapiro's wife was just 40 – the family needed room to expand.

Yehuda and Helen ran a tight Orthodox house.

The nine kids put themselves to bed by 10. The eldest, Shlomo, had a back-breaking entry-level job in the Diamond District. Shlomo was the heir to the jewelry store, the family business, and he was hard-working and earnest. Yehuda believed his oldest son was, over all, a better man than he. Shlomo took supervision of his five younger brothers and three younger sisters seriously. He was the crown jewel of Yehuda and Helen's nine treasures.

Yehuda sat in the small second-story end room that was his study. He checked his e-mail and studied sales reports on his laptop. Helen wandered in.

"Don't stay up late, honey. You don't look so good. Get your rest."

"I'll be there, dear. It's OK."

He sat back down in the dark room, lit by a reading light. He really had no decision to make. There were bills to pay. Lots of people in the community relied on him to take on the responsibility befitting a man of his stature.

"What are you gonna do," he said out loud to himself.

This was nothing, really. Grandfather Shmuel had survived the Holocaust in Bulgaria. Hitler was something to be worried about. These *fakakta* people were just pushy *goyim*. Besides, Ronnie had his back. He got him into this *tsuris*. He would help him get out of it.

Yehuda pushed his brain to another subject: The motorcade. The marriage of the daughter of the rebbe in Montreal to some big *macher* from France required a major presence from the Brooklyn contingent. Yehuda was in charge of coordinating the convoy that would snake up the Brooklyn-Queens Expressway to the New York Thruway and into Canada. At last count, he had 47 vehicles. They would be operated by some of the worst drivers on the East Coast.

Grandfather Shmuel ate grass and acorns for three months as he hid from the Nazis in the forest. This was nothing.

Ross stood outside Flynn's smoking with Laura.

"You're quiet tonight, Walton."

"That's just the booze not talking." Ross was drinking Rolling Rock, but no tequila. Laura was drinking Jack on ice. Laura wore her coat against the October night, but Ross had walked outside in a sweater. A taxi sped down Avenue B, slowed as the driver checked to see if they were potential fares, then shot off.

"Yes, what is up with the not drinking?" She corrected herself. "The hardly drinking."

He took a long drag and exhaled. "My heart's just not in it."

"Oh, dear."

A taxi stopped at the corner. Three young women got out, giggled hilariously at one another and staggered into Flynn's. Laura watched and turned and looked at Ross. She said in her best *Wild Kingdom* voice:

"As the migratory white girls cross into the domain of the urban man-wolf, the predator picks up their scent and follows them to the watering hole."

Ross grinned. "The instinct to pounce is practically overwhelming. But not tonight." Laura made a shocked expression.

"I've been accused of being practically too sad for sex. I've got a karmic block or something." He eyed a thuggish-looking bicyclist who looked a lot like someone he'd arrested a year ago. What did it mean when he saw them again walking around free? Were they rehabilitated? "I need about five weeks of sleep and I'm gonna get it all tonight," he said. "I have a feeling it's a big day tomorrow."

He bid good night to Laura and his other friends at Flynn's. Albert was getting off and wanted Ross to go with him to another bar on Avenue A, but Ross had done that once and woke up the next day with a Top 10 hangover. Going to a bar with an off-duty Irish bartender was like going for a drive in a Porsche with an off-duty Formula One driver.

Albert was a babe magnet, but Ross wasn't in the mood. He wanted the next woman he'd go to bed with to be someone he knew at least a little. Sometimes the object seemed to be to get in and out of bed without learning the first thing about the person you'd been intimate with.

Passing Tompkins Square Park, Ross stopped to light a cigarette and confront the question he'd been running from: Should he quit? Would they ever let him out of the hole in the ground? Was it a lifetime penalty he was serving? What the fuck was the point of twisting in the wind?

Maybe he should go back to Bacciagaloop. Was that why he'd called him in? He thought he could flip Ross to the other side? The old man was still sharp.

******

The corrections officer entered the cluttered little office where inmate Alejandro Cordero counseled fellow convicts.

"Alex, sorry to interrupt, brother, it's that time."

Cordero nodded. "That's OK, Tony. We were just wrapping up." He turned back to the other convict, a burly young man with a shaved head. "Everything bad that happened in my life started with getting high," Cordero said. "Everything." He looked deep into the other man's eyes to let the words register.

"I know, man. I know." The convict's eyes began to well. "You have to help me."

"*You* have to help you," Cordero said. "There's only one way out, and it's through your own soul." He pointed a bony finger at his own chest. "This is where the war is. Inside here." He thumped his chest. "I'm a good man. Without drugs, I'd never set a foot inside this place.

Drugs got me here." His voice grew louder. "Drugs! Drugs! Drugs!" He slapped his hands on the cheap desk. "Are you tough?"

The younger man's prison shirt bulged with prison muscles. "Yeah. You're not tough in here, then you die. You know that, Alex."

"Of course I do. So get tough with yourself. I know what the voices say, 'Just get high, just one last time. *Then* I'll quit.' Well let me tell you something," now Cordero's eyes started to well. His hair was graying. Though he was only 42, he had spent 23 years locked up. The years had moved slowly. "I decided to smoke one last pipe. A farewell buzz. I was 19 and stupid. Got nice and high, and know what?"

"What?"

"When I was done, I wanted more!"

"Yeah."

"So I went out and robbed a man. Took $15 from him. Fifteen motherfucking dollars. Had to stick him to get my dope. But I did it, cause I wasn't tough enough to say no: Here's where I get off this ride.

"This guy was just going along his business. Going home to his wife and kids. I stuck him to get high for an hour. I got an hour of being high, man. He got dead. Died for my high. And after I got done being high, I got caught. I'd stabbed the man around the corner from my own building. How fucking dumb is that?"

"That's messed up."

"Yeah. And now I'm in prison. Murder 2. Life. A fifteen-dollar high, and I paid with the rest of my life. Was it worth it? Kids with no father, me locked up like an animal at the zoo – for drugs?"

"Yeah."

"How long you looking at?"

"Seven to ten. Could get parole in four."

"You're lucky, brother. You get yourself right and you stay far away from here. You go and lead a righteous life. The drug is the enemy. Not the man, not the boss, not the po-leece – the drug."

"Thank you, brother." He embraced Cordero.

Later that night, Cordero lay on his bunk in the dark. Voices and the cacophony of sounds that never ended reverberated through the cell block. Cordero's cell mate, an aging white man from Larchmont who'd had a hitman murder his wife, snored his accompaniment. As he did for each night of the 23 years he'd been locked up, Cordero replayed the murder.

"Give me your wallet."

The man looked confused. He had long hair and a beard. He just stood there.

"Your wallet, motherfucker!"

The man just looked at him. The anger began to build. Cordero remembered the voice in his head. "He's wasting time! You need to get back to the pipe! You need it now!"

Still time to walk away, Cordero thought. Just walk away. Walk.

But his hand held a knife and now it lashed out, punching into the man's gut. He let out a soft cry, more out of surprise than pain.

Now it's too late.

Now you're a killer.

Cordero shut his eyes tightly. This was where he got nauseous. Sometimes he had to throw up.

He opened his eyes again. He was locked up, behind bars, like an animal at the zoo.

Chapter 6

Bouton followed the sign for the 7 train down into the station at Sixth Avenue and 42nd Street. Through the turnstile, he turned left, as directed, down a long dank passage. At 6 a.m., the narrow tube had only light foot traffic: late-night drinkers squinting against the harsh lighting, hardcore Manhattan commuters hurtling toward their desks gripping their briefcases.

He emerged at a staircase and hurried down to catch a departing train. The train stopped at Lexington Avenue to take on a few passengers and let off many more, and continued under the East River to Vernon-Jackson, Bouton's stop, in Queens.

The park was two blocks from the subway, through a neighborhood of crumbling rowhouses that were being overwhelmed by new high-rise condos. Two men working on a battered Taurus in front of an unmarked garage stopped to assess the tall man with ramrod posture as he marched by.

A block from the river, the wind was bitter, and the sun was far too low to do much good. Bouton kept his hands in the pockets of his overcoat.

Bouton was overloaded. The downside of having caught the eye of the President was a cluster of assignments – all high priority. He barely got home to see Mary and the girls. She was a source of endless patience, but she, too, was getting weary of the relentlessness of his responsibilities.

And now he had the hapless Rucker group to contend with. They couldn't seem to get anything right. Bouton resolved to figure out exactly why his betters had insisted on working with these imbeciles. Granted, they needed the contractors to maintain a firewall between black ops and the White House, but Bouton often lay awake the few hours he allotted for sleep wondering which side of that firewall *he* would be in if the shit hit the propeller.

Emerging from a high-rise canyon, Bouton stood at the waterfront and evaluated the gleaming midsection of Manhattan standing like a Broadway set on the other side of the river. Great town, but not for families. A fellow Marine officer once told him, as they rolled over the Kuwaiti desert in search of the Iraqi army, that however much money you had, it was never enough in New York.

A taxi pulled up and Matt North got out. With his gaze on the skyline, he walked over and offered his hand.

"Good morning, Matt."

"Morning, Colonel."

"It's lieutenant colonel, actually, and I pretty much go civilian these days." Bouton could feel the sun break out behind them. They stood side by side, glued to the view. Bouton said nothing. Finally, North spoke.

"It was the Marquezes."

"Uh-huh."

"I used them for supply and logistics."

"Supply and logistics."

"And they did a great job. I'd dealt with them before. I knew people."

"So?"

"The last thing they did was turn around and sell me out to the Venezuelans."

"Why not cash in all the chips."

"Seems that way." They turned to inspect a

passing jogger, a woman wearing a hooded sweatshirt, gloves and gym shorts. "They were waiting for us at the wire."

"Now what? The planes are gone."

"I was hoping you'd tell me," North said. Bouton stared at the younger man.

"This isn't a fucking game. There is interest in this mission at the very top. The *very* top." A ragged man with a two-wheeled cart approached a nearby garbage can and searched for bottles and cans. Bouton and North studied the man carefully.

"I know, Dennis. I fucked up. I admit it. But I know how to go back at this. I've got some things working."

"Some things working."

"Yes. If not for the rat, we were in and out of there and those planes were dust."

Bouton looked across the water at the United Nations to compose himself. He rarely swore, but he didn't care for North and his unctuous, smarmy manner. He didn't trust him.

"In war, there are two kinds of people," Bouton said finally, "those who do, and those who don't. The ones who don't, die. There is no 'if not for.'"

Bouton turned and started marching back to the subway.

******

Ross lived over a pizzeria in a one-bedroom apartment missing such luxuries as dishwasher, air-conditioning and washer/dryer. There was no shower, only a claw foot tub in the ancient kitchen. He had two windows that faced an air shaft. Before Yuppies and well-financed students took over Alphabet City, to lean out the window was to be pelted by garbage as detritus was flung from higher floors. There was a steady supply of roaches, which enjoyed the supply of grease downstairs. Because of all this, the rent was reasonable.

That afternoon, Ross and the backup team started on the Times Square shuttle, which had been experiencing a spate of pickpocketing. Ross' character for the tour was a construction worker with a broken arm. The team rode train after train of law-abiding citizens to Grand Central and back. Ross saw nothing but splendid shoes. They switched to the 7 train from Grand Central, and traveled out to Roosevelt Avenue and back. At Fifth Avenue, they got off to connect with the F train to Brooklyn, home to legions of subway predators.

Ross trailed the three backups as they climbed the steps from the 7 train platform and entered a long, narrow hamster trail of a passageway to the Sixth Avenue end of the station and the F train platform.

"I don't care if the Giants did win the frickin' Super Bowl, that guy is a lousy coach," Gaughan said. "You need good morale to have a good team."

"I hate the Giants," Quinn said. "This is the Jets' year." Ross had no problem looking pained.

It was awkward walking through the crowded tunnel with his unbroken arm. At rush hour, it was as packed as the floor of Madison Square Garden during a Springsteen concert. The occasional hyperactive New York loon cut down the center no-man's land between eastbound and westbound commuters.

Near the midpoint of the tunnel, the westbound walkers were knotted up as they tried to move around a Latina woman who had commandeered valuable floor space for her showroom of bootleg DVDs. Ross had the urge to bust her, but the team rarely broke character except for predators once outside the squad room. On the other side of traffic near where the passage spilled into the Sixth Avenue end of the station, a scruffy man created an extraordinary bottleneck as he butchered Jimi Hendrix on a cheap guitar and an even more primitive amp.

They rode the F train all the way to Stillwell Avenue without observing so much as a cross word. Ross liked the lines like the F and the 7 that climbed out of the ground and afforded riders vistas seen almost exclusively by millionaires living in the city's choicest bits of skyline. As the F train eased into Coney Island, he could see the ocean. This was the point of the ride when the good citizens, no matter how often they had come this way, beheld the magic blue expanse of the Atlantic. It was also the time when the criminals aboard sized up their marks.

As he gazed out to sea, Ross felt eyes on him. On the next row of seats to his right, a thuggish-looking man in a hooded sweatshirt and a backward Mets hat was staring hard at Ross. He looked quickly away, in character as a vulnerable rider with a broken arm. But then he looked back. Monte. He'd busted him for trying to mug him in the Bergen Street station of the G line in January. Monte something. Ross had been in the old man disguise. Why the hell was he back on the street already? The train pulled into Stillwell and Monte quickly melted away.

Crankier than usual from the day's unproductive hunt, the team headed back toward Times Square. Calderon, who lived in Brooklyn, went as far as Park Slope. Ross rode to 42nd Street to grab the 7 to Grand Central and head downtown. Another thrilling day down under. It was an improvement over his grandfather's life as a coal miner in Pennsylvania, he thought, but not by much. His career as a cop had come undone.

At 32, he had 10 years on the force, halfway to the magical 20 and out. He was a golden boy for the first eight, whisked out of uniform and into plainclothes by an instructor whose eye he had caught at the academy. But it came apart in an instant on a subway platform. As in a Greek myth, he was banished underground, to be reminded of his blunder every day, everywhere.

Ross figured there was plenty of time to get downtown and work up a decent buzz at Flynn's. Maybe Leslie would be there and he could have an encore – a happy, cheery fuck that would send her into a giggly Dick

Van Dyke rapture.

He unlocked the quitting option. After suppressing it mightily for at least six months, it popped up now like a jack-in-the-box. He could go upstate, back to Roscoe, and fish and ... and what? He'd be bored shitless. There was always his brother, Keith, out in Oregon. He should at least go check it out. Who knows, if he liked it, what would he need to come back to collect? Not a thing.

Ross bounded up the steps from the F platform and turned into the passageway where, earlier in the day, *Purple Haze* had been mangled. The subway was quiet, except for a Hasid in a long black coat and black hat 50 feet in front of Ross. He wondered why the Hasid would be catching the 7. Weren't they all in Brooklyn?

Ross heard a loud metallic click, then two more, and the Hasid lurched backward, as if pulled by a rope.

He ran ahead just far enough to see around the bend in the tunnel. Beyond the Hasid, Ross saw two men in combat stance. Ross had never heard a silencer shot. Who the fuck uses a silencer? The Hasid fell heavily onto his back.

Ross rushed down the tunnel, fishing his Beretta from his sling. He dropped to one knee and squeezed off five shots. One of the men fell heavily to the ground. He landed on his back and stayed there, motionless. The second gunman and a third man he hadn't noticed at first disappeared at the end of the passageway.

Keeping his gun trained on the fallen man, he advanced. One of Ross' shots had landed dead center in the man's forehead. Several others seemed to have struck his chest. Ross kicked the pistol out of reach anyway.

Ross ran back to the wounded Hasid. He had at least two gurgling chest wounds, but he was conscious. Somehow, his hat was still on his head.

"Who shot you?"

"No one. No one shot me. Leave me alone."

Ross tore the man's shirt open. Three wounds were oozing blood.

"Who shot you?"
"Nobody. Nobody shot me."

Chapter 7

Ross' phone rang at 6:30. He had finally gotten to bed at 5:30, after a four-hour shooting review. This case made the investigators nervous, and they were thorough. The shooter whom Ross had killed was named Tony Bozzo. He was from Canarsie, but had seen the world as a Navy SEAL and then returned to New York to practice privately what the military had trained him to do expertly.

The call was from William Herron, the deputy commissioner for intelligence and Ross' rabbi on the NYPD.

"Sorry to call so early," he said. "The review went fine. We need to discuss the case. Meet me at 9 at the ferry dock in Battery Park. OK, Ross?"

"Um," Ross' eyes were still closed and he was trying to summon up a voice. "OK, yes sir. Battery Park, 9 o'clock. You got it."

"Seeya."

Ross had shot a couple of people in the line of work, but he'd never killed one. He was surprised to find that he felt just fine with it. Otherwise, what was the point of all that weapons training?

The interrogation the night before had established that he had made the good play. He had told them his impulses as a cop had taken over. Simple, really. Now, as he jogged to the subway, the words *Navy SEAL* reverberated in his head. What had he stepped in?

Ross spotted Herron waiting by the seawall, wearing a trench coat and looking like a tall, lanky spy. A razor wind blew in from the water. The ferry from Liberty Island was a dot steadily plowing through white-capped chop.

They shook hands.

"How have you been, Ross?"

"Good, sir. Hanging in. Thanks for asking."

"Why don't I buy that?"

A dozen responses came to mind, but Ross just shrugged,

"This is a juicy one," Herron began. "The vic is a Hasidic Diamond District jeweler named Yehuda Shapiro. We've got nothing on him. He's still saying no one shot him, which is what I would say if I were him. *Someone* shot him three times. Two shots hit his right lung, and he would have died in 10 minutes if you hadn't come along." A gull screamed toward shore and they both turned to watch it.

"Is he going to make it?" Ross asked.

"Not a chance. Just a matter of when."

They stood by the sea wall, looking out at the water.

"So far, the SEAL is going nowhere," Herron said. "He lives in Brooklyn, so his ATM withdrawals and credit card charges tell us nothing. We're still working the calls on his cell phone. If I needed to hit somebody professionally, this guy would be near the top of my list."

Ross nodded. A homeless man wandered over to beg, but moved off when the two hard-eyed men glared at him.

"Why would someone order up a hit on this guy?" Herron asked. Ross could now make out the people on the ferry. He had put on a lined denim jacket that was not much of a match for the sea breeze.

"Not mob. They have their own talent." Herron shook his head in agreement. "My guess would be another Hasid. They get a little crazy in their business dealings. Some of the community politics get out of hand, too." They had been looking out to sea, but now Herron put a hand on Ross' shoulder and looked him in the eye.

"I want you to work this," he said. Ross stared, then looked away. The homeless man was working the businessmen carrying their attaché cases through the park.

"I don't think I'd be very much use to you. I'm not well-liked in the department these days."

"Forget the department. I want you to report directly to me on this. If anyone else in the department asks you about it, send them to me. We'll keep this off the books." Ross said nothing.

"Don't be an idiot, Ross. This is your chance to redeem yourself. There are a lot of cops I could choose from, but I picked you for this one." The ferry approached the dock and they stopped to watch it land. "This smells very bad, and I need you to straighten it out before some other pro takes someone out in a public place. This is New York, not Tombstone."

"Thank you, sir." They shook hands. "I won't let you down."

"I know you won't." Herron walked off.

Ross lit a cigarette. The sun climbed over some clouds and took the chill off.

******

Not good, not good at all, Matt North thought as he labored through his exercise regimen in his hotel room. He raged at the incompetence of the three assassins through his 30th pushup. Two, actually, since Bozzo was now dead. They hadn't seemed like fuckups down in the Amazon.

By pushup 45, he had turned the corner, and was thinking of his next move. When he hit 75 to finish the set, he was calm. This was a jam, but nothing worse than what he'd faced in Colombia with the Agency. Wasn't it just a week ago when he'd walked out of the jungle? The logistics had been wonderful. He'd made it out.

Dennis Bouton could kiss his ass. The guy was ripe for an aneurysm. Washington did strange things to people. He'd had a good friend in Colombia who'd come out of the field for a desk job at Langley. In six months, his friend was insufferable – fat, bloated, gray, devoid of life.

North started on his crunches and considered the worst-case scenario: His two mercs could be arrested. But they were pros. The chances they would flip on him were low.

North began his kata, firing punches toward his mirror image, blocking, spinning and kicking. When he was done, he felt his confidence flowing again. The job would be simpler with just the two of them. They would finish quickly, quietly, neatly and leave town. And he'd never use them again.

He examined his upper body in the mirror: All lean muscle. There was no way he could fail. Suddenly he was eager to be back in Houston. He didn't need to be on site for the next series of events. He'd give strict instructions and fly back.

Back to her.

******

Police Commissioner Jack Steele looked like a bulldog. Massive sloping shoulders ascended to a stump of a neck. He wore a military-style brush cut. His eyes squinted when he was skeptical. His eyes were squinting now.

"Why this guy Walton?" the commissioner asked.

"I've known him since he hit the Academy," Herron said. "He's a battler. You'd have to kill this guy; he won't quit. And he's smart. He's got the brain to operate on his own. Remember the Lisa Santiago case?"

"In Bushwick? The little girl who was —"

"Yes. Raped and strangled. Disgusting crime. The

Mayor's office was all over us. Top of the 11 o'clock news for weeks. Ross was working Brooklyn Major Cases. He never left the neighborhood for three days. Talked to every junkie and skel out there. Slept two nights in crack houses. He busted loose the lead and made the collar."

"I remember now. That was terrific work."

"He used a makeup kit to slip into crack houses. Looked like he belonged."

Steele's computer clicked with the arrival of an e-mail message. He craned his neck to inspect it but dismissed it with the shake of his large head.

"Look, he's driven," Herron continued. "His father was killed in a street robbery when he was a kid. He's not a 20-and-out guy from Long Island. He's from the neighborhood. He grew up with the wiseguys and he's wired to the street."

"Well, he definitely has balls. Two years on subway decoy with a big kick-me sign on his back. He's a tough kid."

"It's time to get him out of there," said Herron. "He'll be a valuable asset. Otherwise, we'll lose him."

"How can he handle this on his own?"

"He won't have to. I've got someone to partner him with. A woman with a very interesting background. CIA-trained, weapons expert, tournament-level martial arts expertise."

"A woman?"

"Believe me, this is someone who commands attention."

Steele leaned back in his big leather chair. "I hate to even say this." Herron nodded his head. "But this operation stays in your shop. It doesn't come up to this office."

"That's the thing," Herron said. "For this to work, this is not a police job. He's operating on spy rules. We need results, not nice, tidy cases for the DA."

"Yeah," said Steele. "Hizzoner's Secret Service."

Chapter 8

Ross called Sammy but got his voicemail – "This is Sammy. Don't leave a message. I don't return calls. Call me later; maybe you'll get lucky." He headed up to the bar that was more or less Sammy's office on Grand Street.

It was nearly 9 by the time he got there, having walked to give him a chance to rerun the conversation with Herron several dozen times. *We'll keep this off the books ... This is New York, not Tombstone.* I'm in a world of shit I don't even know about, he thought. But then he flashed to his last shift in the subway and realized it was his *last* shift in the subway. He savored even the diesel-scented fresh air of TriBeCa.

Ross swung open the door to Sammy's bar. Once his eyes adjusted to the darkness, he spotted Sammy at a table in the back of the long, narrow bar room. He was deep in conversation, but he noticed Ross and gestured to the bar. Ross sat on a stool and asked for a double espresso. He'd have to power load caffeine to make it through the day.

Sammy's confederate finally got up and walked straight out of the bar.

"Ros-coe!" Sammy yelled, summoning him to the table in the back. They shook hands. Sammy looked like a Mafioso: Thick mustache, jet-black unkempt hair, piercing dark eyes. Roman nose, artistically bent to the right. Ross had punched that nose before the two street kids decided to be friends.

"You and my mother are the only ones who call me that," Ross said.

"I only call you that because that's your fucking name."

"True, true. How's business, Sam? No wait. I don't want to know." Sammy laughed.

"Hey, anyone tell you recently that you look like shit?" Sammy said.

"Just you, Sammy." He looked over Sammy's attire. "You look, ah, prosperous." Sammy was wearing a gray sharkskin suit. He tugged on the knot of his thin Cardin tie. Most mob guys dressed like the bums at the OTB.

"It's a Giovanelli."

"A what?"

"This suit is vintage, my man." Sammy called to the man who had served the espresso. "Yo, Johnny, bring us a couple of XOs." Johnny nodded.

"Woe, Sam, it's like 10 in the morning," Ross said.

"So? When's the last time we got drunk early in the morning? Probably when you went into the police academy, pardon the expression. Now I'm in *the life*, and you're in … the life." He made the second *the life* sound like a diagnosis of lung cancer. Johnny brought over two snifters.

Ross poked his nose into the glass. "What is this stuff?"

Sammy spoke to Johnny, who was about twice the age of Sammy. "This is an old, old friend of mine. Not a friend of *ours*" – the three laughed – "but a good man, even if he happens to be on the payroll of a certain city agency that shall go nameless. This is Ross Walton. He was a hick from the sticks upstate somewhere, but damned if he wasn't the toughest kid in the Wilson Houses."

"Nice to meet ya, Ross." Johnny returned to his work station.

"This is Hennessy XO. Smoother than J-Lo's ass."

"Nice." Ross took a sip and left it on his tongue. "Very nice. But I can't get wasted. I'm working above ground again, starting now."

"Hey, that's good. It's unhealthy down there, aside from the *moulanyan* smacking you in the head. I'd still like to see you in another line of work. But that's me." He took a slug of XO. "How's your mom? I miss her, the tough old bird."

Ross laughed. "She's doing OK. Terrorizing her neighbors. They don't have many Sicilians in Roscoe. I'll tell her you said hi."

"Remember when that old hag threw the pitcher of water at us for playing ball under her window?"

"You mean the water pitcher. She threw the fucking glass pitcher at us."

"What?" asked Johnny from the bar.

"Yeah, crazy bitch," said Sammy. He and Ross began to giggle. "She could have killed us. We were like—"

"Twelve," said Ross. "I think we were twelve." They began to laugh harder.

"Mamalukie."

"Yes! Fucking Mamalukie. What was her actual name? Did anyone know?" Sammy shrugged, and doubled over.

"Your mom grabbed her by the hair and popped her. Boom! Right in the fucking eye. Crack! She had knuckle prints on her head." Even Johnny began to laugh.

"You don't cross Mom," said Ross.

Sammy tilted his head back and drained his drink.

"So let me guess," he said, "you want to play the name game."

"You got it."

"Let's take a walk." They walked down Grand and turned north on Thompson. It had continued to warm up and old Italian men were sipping espresso at sidewalk tables as trucks inched their way down the block spewing black exhaust.

"Yehuda Shapiro, Diamond District jeweler," Ross said. Sammy stopped walking.

"Don't know him," Sammy said.

"Why don't I buy that?"

"I don't give a fuck what you buy."

"What if I told you he got popped in the subway last night, right in front of me, by some mercenaries?"

"*Are* you telling me that?" Sammy started walking again.

"Yeah. I capped one of them. Guy named Bozzo from Canarsie."

"Fuck." Sammy turned down Broome Street. He lit a cigarette and so did Ross. "You didn't get it from me, bro."

"Of course." A very tall blond in a very short skirt passed them and they stopped to consider her aesthetic qualities.

"*Marrone*," Sammy whispered. It was his highest compliment. "OK. This Shapiro was working with the Colombians. They sell their cocaine and what-not and they have piles and piles of cash. Only it's not so easy moving the cash back to the home office. So Shapiro takes their cash and turns it into gold."

"What do you mean *gold*?"

"Gold. Actual gold. They buy gold and he makes shit out of it. Gold tools, gold pots and pans, gold butt plugs – I don't know, ordinary shit. They paint it to look like aluminum or whatever and Customs doesn't give two shits."

"That's fucking brilliant."

"Yeah, they liked it. Back there, they melt it down again and sell the gold. Now they've got more capital for more coke and suddenly the business is 100 times better than ever."

"So, rule out the Colombians for whacking the

guy."

"Believe me, they don't need freelance killers. They could teach us a thing or two." They turned the corner at West Broadway, headed back to the bar.

"Get the fuck outta here!" Sammy suddenly growled. He pointed at a homeless man sitting cross-legged in the doorway of a bakery. "I caught this guy taking a shit in front of the bar last week," he said to Ross. "Can you fucking believe that? What is this city coming to?"

"Hey!" he yelled at the man. "What did I tell you?" The man began to get up but wasn't quick enough to avoid being kicked by one of Sammy's vintage shoes. "I catch you around here again I'll cement your ass shut." The man hustled down the street. "Go back to Newark, ya sidewalk-shittin' cocksucker!"

He turned back to Ross, blank faced.

"Shapiro," Ross reminded him.

"Oh, right. Here's the interesting part: I needed to trade something to the FBI to resolve a certain matter. I gave them Shapiro. 'Uh-uh,' they say. 'Not interested in that.' Now why do you suppose that is?"

******

"Good morning, Mr. President."

"Good morning, Andrea, Dennis. Please have a seat."

Dennis Bouton and his boss, Andrea Hopkins, national security adviser to the President, sat on one of the two matching Oval Office couches. President James H. Morgan sat opposite them.

"Somalia," said the President.

"Yes sir," Hopkins said, beginning the briefing. "The government is besieged. Their Interior minister, as you know, was assassinated last week and the Somalis are claiming extremists from other countries are responsible. The Agency concludes, and I concur, that the threat is from domestic warlords, as it has been since our own ill-fated occupation there."

"So we're not in danger of it becoming a big al-Qaeda petri dish?" asked the President.

"Not at the moment, no," said Hopkins.

"But as you realize, sir," Bouton interjected, "it is a tough place to find human assets. The NSA has been able to gather a tremendous amount of data and they're utilizing a great deal of manpower to analyze it. It's a hairy situation. Even in Mogadishu, the government has very little hold."

"Sir, we could prepare a memorandum looking at our strategy options here," Hopkins offered.

"Dennis," said the President. "Can you be the difference maker here? Throw that on your plate?"

"Of course, sir."

"I know you have a lot on your plate – South America, and so forth – but we need to be ahead of this."

"I understand, sir."

"And speaking of … our South American friend," the President said, steering the briefing to one of his favorite subjects, President Antonio Gallegos de la Paz of Venezuela, "I understand he's now shopping for battleships."

"Yes sir," said Bouton. "The Pentagon is estimating now that the Gallegos regime will top out at $3 billion in military hardware purchasing this year – mainly fighter jets, but also transport and attack helicopters and about 100,000 small arms. They are projecting, however, that due to the fall in oil prices, their spending is certain to come down."

"Well I don't like it," the President said. "Gallegos is a vulgar dictator. His elections are fixed, he lets his people live in despair while he spreads money around South America like a rich uncle. Whatever we're for, he's against. Our enemies are his friends."

The President got up and began to pace. "He's too close to us and has too much money to be allowed to continue to turn our own hemisphere against us." He shook his head in disgust. "I won't stand for it!" The President was practically shouting. Bouton noticed the Secret Service agent stationed outside beyond the French doors of the Oval Office staring in. "Pull out all the stops for this … miscreant."

"Yes sir," Hopkins said. "Dennis has some well-focused programs in operation. We have some options here for sure."

"Good. He's no goddamned Robin Hood. He's a gangster with an oil well."

Bouton and Hopkins nodded their heads in agreement.

******

They retreated to Hopkins' office in the Old Executive Office Building.

"He's really losing it over Gallegos," Hopkins said.

"I noticed."

She shook her head sadly. "Now the State Department is upset. The Venezuelans called in our ambassador to read him the riot act over the raid. Of course, he had no clue what they were talking about. Just as well. Not much we can say there."

"Are they booting him?"

She shook her head. "Who knows? Wouldn't be the first time. Whoever's posted in Caracas has to keep a bag packed."

"I know we've talked about this before, but there's nothing the Agency can do?"

She put her hand on top of her head and stretched her neck. "I need a spa weekend," she said, and smiled wearily.

"The government should have civil service massage therapists," Bouton said. "They would pay for themselves."

"Nice thought. Anyway, we're concerned Congress would get wind and clamp down on anything the Agency attempted. Remember the Contras and the Boland Amendment? I don't think we want to go down that road again. And the other problem is all the noise whenever the Agency puts together an op."

"Everyone hears about it."

"Pretty near, yes. They need to send cables if they order lunch. If we handle this with contractors, it just appears to be another operator finding some weapons or planes – a little private military job – not the U.S. government hanging out a big 'help wanted' sign."

She grabbed a bottle of water from behind her desk and gestured to Bouton, but he waved "no."

"What they can do is provide intel, which is always useful, while we seed the clouds."

"Seed the clouds?"

"Yes, encourage the resistance. We know they're there. We have to keep pushing it – your work will embolden them."

"Exactly. They're there. We know it. We need to encourage them."

Chapter 9

Ross was about to fall over from exhaustion. He was trying to determine if it would be more beneficial to get a couple hours of sleep or guzzle some coffee and read the papers at Flynn's, then head out to Canarsie. In the back of his brain – or maybe it was the other side – he was still digesting what Sammy had told him: Shapiro and the Colombians had a free pass from the FBI. Somewhere in there, someone was doing government work.

He tried to remember what he had seen the night before. Was there some telltale sign of who the silencer-shooting gunmen were? Not a chance. He was too far away, and too preoccupied with the silencer, the falling Hasid, and whether they were going to return fire at him.

Nobody shot me. What the fuck was that supposed to mean? The guy was supposed to whisper a clue while the life was draining out of him – "Mickey did it, the rat bastard." Had he done something to justify being murdered without a protest?

Ross passed a Starbucks on Prince Street and considered going in for a monstrous-sized cup of strong coffee – make it Colombian! – and that's when he noticed the two white men following him. The smaller one was about six foot and 200 pounds and seemed to be made of granite. The second one was NFL lineman size. Each had heads of hair that looked like buzz cuts that were growing in. They looked like mechanized humans. Like ... Navy SEALS.

He turned east on Prince; they turned east on Prince. They were lousy at surveillance, unless being undetected was unimportant. King Kong didn't exactly blend into the environment.

At Wooster Street, Ross stopped for traffic and the hulks closed the gap. Ross darted in front of a speeding taxi that squealed its brakes and honked long and hard. His tails weren't very good at walking in New York.

They were half a block behind when the light turned and they were able to cross. Ross let them close the gap enough so that he could see their reflections in the storefront windows. He adjusted his pace to just make the light at Mercer Street, leaving them stranded again on the other side of a maniacal stream of traffic. Looking over his shoulder, he saw them fuming at the curb.

If he could lead them back to Bacciagaloop's, he thought, he and Sally Beans could make short work of them.

Sally was an evil fucker. Ross remembered when Sally caught up with a guy who was way behind on his loan payments, Sally lifted the guy over his head and threw him down on a spike-topped wrought-iron gate. Ross hadn't been there at the time, but Sammy had knocked on his door with the news and they ran down to see the guy squirming and shrieking on the fence. Firemen had to saw off the top of it to get him out of there. Sally got his money.

Ross dawdled again, to let them catch up. At Broadway, he went down into the subway station, but crossed over to the exit on the east side and popped back up on the street. They stared from across the street; they hadn't taken the bait. Ross turned north on Crosby. They were beginning to jog.

At Jersey Street, no bigger than an alley, Big and Bigger caught up.

"Buddy, got the time?" the lineman asked. Few

people who ask that question in New York are interested in the answer. Always take out the biggest one first – he'd learned that as a kid on the playground. Ross threw a right hook that connected high on the big man's left jaw. It was a knockout punch for most of humanity. The giant tumbled to the ground. Ross turned to face the other attacker but felt a kick explode into his right side. The big guy was back on his feet now and moved in as Ross doubled over. He clubbed the back of Ross' head with a brick-sized fist.

Ross collapsed to the sidewalk, his side white hot and his brain pan reverberating. His left side lit up with pain as another kick struck him. He looked up to see a muscled arm holding a thick-bladed hunting knife. A boot found the side of his head with force and for a moment, everything turned white. Then a whirl of blond hair, masculine grunts, feminine shrieks, the thud of kicks and punches, bodies falling around him to the ground.

******

Ross heard talking. A woman with an unusually pleasing voice. "You OK?" she wanted to know. "Is anybody home?" He thought about opening his eyes, but figured that could wait. Pain radiated up and down his body. Ross had nothing but stupid questions in his head. What season was it? He felt neither warm nor cold. What month was it? He began an internal audit of moving and essential parts – left arm? Check. Right leg? Check.

"Is anybody home?" The voice again. He opened his eyes to address the voice and stared into the sapphire eyes of the blond who had passed him and Sammy on Broome Street.

"*Marrone*," he told her, in a voice that didn't sound like his.

In between noticing that she was tall, very, very blond and had a face at once sturdy and delicate – a splash of freckles, cheekbones and lips that belonged on a movie screen – he realized he was lying in an alley somewhere downtown. He was sure of downtown, but was it summer? Spring? Why was that so hard to figure out?

He found it hard to focus any of his thoughts. What was that drink recipe? Quarter-glass of Old Bushmill's, lime juice. Something else. Shake. Stir? Maybe blend.

The nose was sleek and fair, like the rest of her. She wrinkled that nose and asked: "You gonna live?"

******

He heard voices again. This time it was a man with a deep voice and his nice new friend, the blond. He liked freckles. He wanted to open his eyes and see her again. He had so much to live for now. But wait, the beating. Somehow nothing hurt. That didn't seem right. He felt refreshed. Had he made it home to sleep?

"Well obviously he needed some looking after." This was the man's voice. "He's never come up against mercs."

"That was quite the ass kicking." The nice voice. "If we're going to work together, I'll have to train him. He's pretty useless against pros." Ross opened his eyes.

"I heard that," Ross said slowly. "You called me useless."

She walked to his side. "This *is* a hospital bed you're lying in."

Tired, very tired. Ross drifted back to sleep.

******

Lyle Rucker sat in his study watching oil prices on the spot market. Not that Aero Exploration had any surplus to sell; God knows he needed more wells. Growth was stagnant. A curse on the Prius. Didn't those electric car idiots know how much blood and guts went into building an oil company?

Fortunately, Rucker had no children to leave a dying business. He hadn't had the nerve to have children after Meg passed. What sense did it make for a 25-year-old woman to die of leukemia? What could the Good Lord have been thinking? On their second wedding anniversary, Rucker, still only 27, was standing beside her freshly dug grave. No, life was too frail to chance bringing children into the world.

He'd married a second time and it cost him dearly to get that shrew out of his life. He'd waited a good long while before committing to Debbie. But she was a keeper. He'd rest for all eternity knowing Debbie was enjoying his fortune – whatever was left of it.

Debbie swept in wearing a dark blue gown. Her golden hair tumbled over bare shoulders. Hours invested by the pool had produced a mild bronze.

"Good Lord, girl," said Rucker. "Let me catch my breath."

Debbie smiled – the wholesome smile she had aimed at thousands of football fans thinking unwholesome thoughts. "Thank you, sugar." She wandered over to Rucker and stood over his shoulder. Her perfume smelled expensive.

"Tell me what this is again that we're going to?" she asked.

"It's a fund-raiser for Reverend Nesmith's worldwide mission. The usual crowd of scheming multimillionaires."

"Oh yes," Debbie purred. "Them." She leaned down and touched her cheek to Rucker's. Now he would spend the evening thinking of the moment when they arrived back at their sprawling home. He would peel off the expensive gown and worship the bronzed flesh – his 72 virgins in the here and now.

"Hmm, spot market's down," she said.

"Yes, but we've got nothing to sell."

"But what about buying on the dips?" She nibbled

his ear. "Zig when they're all zagging. Isn't that what you always say, sugar?"

Rucker drew back to behold his young wife. "Well look at you!"

Chapter 10

Det. Lt. Ron Margolis put his pants on. He looked out the window of the row house, a cheap cab fare from La Guardia in Queens, to see that it had started to rain gently.

"Te gusta?" Sonia asked.

"Si, me gusto mucho," he replied.

Sonia, brown-eyed and petite, was his preferred partner when he visited the brothel run by the Marquez brothers, who had built a large fortune in the international drug trade. Margolis had put in his 20 years and could have retired with a police pension, but there were so many fringe benefits for a veteran detective who understood the ebb and flow of the underworld.

Thanks to Margolis' Colombian patrons, his daughter had earned a Bachelor's degree from Colgate University. His twin sons had just started at Penn with similar tuition assistance. In what other line of work would you find clients eager to pay for your children's education and ensure that your libido is satisfied as well? You'd be lucky enough just to get health insurance.

Margolis left the brothel thinking of Sonia's many talents. Not the least of them was being 150 pounds smaller than his wife, the mother of his three children, the mound at the other end of his bed. Diane was physically incapable of performing some of the acts at which Sonia, with her luminous smile, excelled; his wife's repertory had been limited even before her over-enlargement.

The brothel was not a house of prostitution in the usual sense; the guests were all those whom the Marquezes wanted to keep in their good graces. Money never changed hands. The managers were careful never to expose one guest to another. Margolis never saw anyone who didn't work there, but he understood that the clientele consisted of other important cops, judges, Customs officials and various inspectors and officials at Kennedy Airport. Instead of a goody bag at the end of the free dinner, they got an unimaginably exhilarating sexual experience.

As one of the stars of the Manhattan North Homicide Squad, Margolis was a 600-pound gorilla in the NYPD. His record at solving some of the most heinous crimes in the city, in one of its toughest districts, was such that the Manhattan chief of detectives and the brass at Police Plaza gave him the kind of latitude a weak government might give a warlord.

Margolis had settled into a routine whenever he visited Sonia – or one of her delectable colleagues – of stopping for coffee, an English muffin and the papers at the Kiwi Diner on Astoria Boulevard on his way down Grand Central Parkway to the Triborough Bridge. The half hour gave him a chance to gather energy and focus for a day of confronting the stone killers of Upper Manhattan.

His thoughts turned to Yehuda Shapiro. The poor schmuck was in way over his head. Margolis had tried to warn him, but the jeweler hadn't learned to control his greed. Too bad he had to be sacrificed. But Margolis' matchmaking had earned him valuable points with the Marquezes and $75,000 from Matt North, wired quietly into his offshore account. No doubt whomever North reported to now knew that Ron Margolis was the man to see to get things done in New York.

Margolis eased his Crown Victoria onto the parkway at 94th Street and flipped on WINS, the all-news station. The radio spat out the headlines:

"Mayor Silva seeks new limits on contractors. A Diamond District jeweler has died a day after being shot in the subway. The Yanks entertain the Sox in the ALCS at the Stadium."

Oh shit, he thought. The dumb yid.

Once Margolis got to the diner, he saw that the newspapers were running down the blind alley of a business deal gone bad as the motive for the shooting. He was sure the flacks at Police Plaza were feeding the erroneous coverage. Whatever made a good story was good enough to keep the press busy until the truth could be determined.

His friends downtown had told him that the cop who had stumbled across the shooting in progress – that kid who got his ass in the ringer for accidentally shooting a black undercover in the subway a couple of years ago – was on the case. He felt secure.

Margolis flipped to the back page of *The Daily News*. There was turmoil among the Yankees. People pay *money* for this information? Margolis finished his coffee and collected his papers. He left a nice tip; he always did.

"Bye, hon," the girl at the counter said. He winked. He felt debonair and dashing, powerful and wise. Wealthy. Virile. On top.

The rain had stopped and the clouds were reverse-commuting to Long Island. He slid into the Crown Vic, closed the door and turned the key. He never heard the engine turn over. He never heard the click of the silencer.

Jason "Ironhead" Hummel eased the Silver Pathfinder out of its parking spot when he saw the contents of Margolis' skull paint the windshield of the Crown Victoria. Michael McKenzie, Hummel's team leader from their Green Beret days in Afghanistan, slowly stepped from the backseat of Margolis' car. He locked the door and walked unrushed to the Pathfinder.

Hummel pulled onto Astoria Boulevard and quickly turned north on 37th Street, lest they get stuck in the inching traffic near 31st Street.

"Piece of cake, huh, Skip?" Hummel said.

"I'm starving," McKenzie said, "but let's find another diner."

******

The Rev. John Stanton Nesmith tucked a napkin into his shirt. Any misaimed lunch would have to defy gravity and take the long way around his rotund midsection to land in his lap.

Tom Catapano tried to ignore the gorging going on across the table. Part of his portfolio as senior counselor to the President was to attend to the Reverend Nesmiths of the world who kept the campaigns flush with capital.

"So I found myself spending so much time in Washington, between ministry business and political what-have-you, that we finally broke down and bought this condo," the reverend said. He ladled more gravy onto a mound of mashed potatoes. "I had some misgivings about being in the Watergate – all those dark Nixon associations – but golly the view sure is nice, ain't it?"

"It's breathtaking, truly breathtaking," Catapano said sincerely. The room had a floor-to-ceiling wall of glass that afforded an expansive view of the Potomac, the marina and the Key Bridge. "This is very tranquil, and tranquility is hard to find in this town." Catapano smiled broadly.

"Well I truly appreciate your taking the time from your busy schedule to have lunch with a fat old fool," the reverend said.

Catapano laughed charmingly. "Reverend I can agree with the busy schedule part, but I don't know about the rest of that. I do hope you know, though, that the President appreciates all you've done for us."

"Of course, of course," the reverend said. Servers cleared the plates quickly, aware that the reverend did not like to keep dessert waiting. "And I do have a favor to ask."

"Shoot," said Catapano.

"The ministry would like to give our God's Love Award to the President. There's a dinner in Houston. With the President there, we could sell 2,500 tickets at 10K a pop. That adds up to a few dollars. And the ministry would be most generous when campaign time rolled around." The two were served massive slabs of layer cake. "Think about it, Tom. I don't want to put you on the spot."

Catapano grinned. "Spot? What spot?" Charming, always smiling, even at hopeless situations. Without Catapano, James H. Morgan would be keynoting Elks Club dinners in Bangor. "He'll be there. He's going to be thrilled." He studied the cake and wondered how long it would take to burn off this gluttony. Catapano cut a dashing figure around town, frequently escorting women who were both ravishing and intellectual. A dangling gut would be the undoing of the image he had carefully crafted.

"Thank you, sir. You are too kind." The reverend sugared his coffee. "By the way, Lyle Rucker is quite taken with Matt North. He's a very clever young man."

Chapter 11

Ross awoke in a nice private room at Bellevue, hospital of choice for injured New York cops. Herron was there but Ross focused first on blond goddess.

"So I lived?" he said.

"Appears so," she said. Herron walked into view.

"Ross, meet Tori Anderson. I thought you'd need a backup. She figured she could be more effective if you didn't know she was there. As you know now, she can handle herself."

"Yeah," Ross said, "she handles others pretty well, too." Tori smirked. "Thanks. You a cop?" he asked.

"No. The Agency. But we had a difference of opinions. I work freelance now." A young Indian doctor entered the room.

"Hello," he nodded to Tori and Herron, then addressed himself to Ross. "I am Dr. Pradesh. Your injuries are very slight. Ribs, just bruised, not broken. You've had a bad knock in the head. Concussion of the second-degree. You lost consciousness, yes?" He held Ross' eyelids open and inspected his pupils with a penlight.

"Yeah, that's what they tell me."

"Fine, very fine." Ross' pupils passed the test. "You have a contusion on the back of the head. Apply ice to relieve the swelling. And avoid striking your head.

Otherwise, if you have someone who can monitor you for the next 24 hours for signs of brain injury – which I think you are lacking – you can dress and leave here." He scribbled on a pad and handed Ross a prescription. "Percocet for the pain."

"Yum," Ross said. Dr. Pradesh hurried out.

"Meet your new partner," Herron said. Ross squinted his eyes in confusion. Herron twisted his head in Tori's direction.

"Must be my lucky day," Ross said.

"Yeah, well, we'll see," Tori said.

"Look," Herron told Ross, "whoever ordered the hit on Shapiro ordered you taken out as well. That means they have more work to do, and it would be easier to do without you to worry about."

"I'd bet that work involves more murder or a very loud bang," Tori said.

"Either would be bad," Herron said. Ross felt a little slow processing this information, but otherwise none the worse for his near-fatal beating. He remembered a large knife, but apparently Tori had squashed that idea.

"So we need to follow the thugs back to the nest and kill the queen," Ross said. Herron and Tori stared as if to read Ross' thought bubble. "So this isn't really police work," he concluded.

Herron crossed his arms and leaned back against the wall. "We need to see where this goes," he said. "Goal No. 1 is to keep the city safe. You'll be going up against highly trained people. It's not the subway; you won't be able to wrestle them down and slap cuffs on them. If you don't use deadly force, they'll kill you."

Ross looked from Herron to Tori. "I get the picture," he said.

Tori insisted Ross stay with her at the apartment Herron had provided near Columbus Circle. If mercenaries were tracking him, no use making it easy. He was not about to argue.

The apartment was a fourth-floor walkup on West

58th Street, across from Roosevelt Hospital's back door. A tiny bedroom was linked by a long hallway and galley kitchen to an even tinier living room with a sofa bed. No more than 500 square feet for two people. It seemed like heaven for Ross. A steady stream of ambulances landed across the way, and their flashing lights made it seem as if they were camped at a crime scene.

"First thing," Tori said, once he'd settled in and they'd sat down to talk on the sleep sofa, "I will not sleep with you."

"You're not my type," Ross said. Tori smiled. "OK, you're everybody's type. Sorry, I lied. I'd shoot myself in the knee to sleep with you. But no sleeping. Lewd thoughts maybe, but no, um, touching." Tori narrowed her eyes. "But if we're going to be partners, the important thing is we have to be honest with each other."

"Fine," she said. "I don't pull any punches."

"Yeah, I noticed back there. What was that, jujitsu?"

"Maybe. A little of everything. My parents put me in a taekwondo program when I was 4, growing up in Denver. A little dojang run by two tiny women who could rip your head off with two fingers. It's always been like breathing for me. I won a national tournament when I was in college, and that's when the Agency found me."

"The CIA? What did you do for them?"

She scrunched up her face and said in a faux gangster voice: "If I told you, I'd have to kill you."

"Yeah, OK, but could we sleep together first?"

They ordered Chinese takeout and resolved that Tori would train Ross in the basics of useful street fighting. Ross, slurping greasy moo shoo pork from the carton, told his most descriptive account of Shapiro's killing, and his bull's-eye in the foreheard of Tony Bozzo. In the division of labor, Ross would do the shooting.

"I'm a little confused," Tori said, "Why you? Out of all the cops in New York, why do they trust *you* with this? I mean, as far as I can tell, you're kind of worthless."

Ross slumped back on the sofa and studied the ceiling. His head hurt. "I used to be a smart cop. I was the golden boy."

"Hmm," Tori said. "Like, what did you do that was so special?"

Ross shot her a look.

"No, seriously. What was your best case? Your finest hour?"

His ribs hurt, so he spoke without turning toward her.

"I got decorated for this one case. A little girl in Brooklyn. Some drugged-out perv grabbed her and – it was pretty bad. I saw her body at the crime scene. I wasn't going to leave the neighborhood without the scumbag that had done it."

"And you got him."

"Yeah, I got him." It seemed like a lifetime before the subway. Was he really done down there?

"Are you leaving the good part out? Or is that it?"

"I had a girlfriend at the time who was on Broadway. Ensemble stuff. She had a friend of hers, a makeup artist, work on me. I looked like a stone crackhead. I wandered the neighborhood for three days, spent two nights in a crack house. No one wanted to get involved, but they didn't mind gossiping to me cause I was just another skel."

"Skel?"

"The walking dead. Barely human. A skeleton."

"So who did it?"

"A skel. He got good and high and decided what he needed was to fuck some innocent kid. Right then, this little girl came walking around the corner. She was nine years old."

"That's horrible."

He turned to her, just his head. "Yeah. I knew I'd get him. It was just a matter of time. One guy knew a guy who knew a guy who said something about something. I worked the chain of dirtbags. A normal cop with a cheap suit and a marine haircut wasn't going to make that bust."

"Impressive work."

Ross frowned. "Yeah, well, that was a few years ago."

He looked quizzically at Tori. "And why, I should ask, would you agree to work with such a fuckup as myself?"

She cupped her chin in her hand and said, "I need someone to watch my back." She yawned, stood and stretched to her full six feet. "Time for sleep," she said.

"I was just going to offer a foot massage," Ross said.

"Don't make me put you back in the hospital."

******

Bacciagaloop shook his head.

"A broad saved him?"

"That's what the kid said," Sammy told him.

"Get the fuck outta here," said Sally Beans.

Bacciagaloop puffed his cigar. He and Sammy sipped their grappa. Sally drank Diet Coke. He avoided alcohol and spicy food since the mid-'70s, when he was shot in the stomach.

"And this broad kicked the shit outta the two *cafones*?" the old man asked.

"That's what the kid said."

"Get the fuck outta here," said Sally.

Sammy wished he were anywhere else, preferably in the sack with the Chinese chick from next door.

"*Marrone*," said the old man. "Maybe we should hire *her*. How is he?"

"He don't sound too bad. I woulda gone to see him except the hospital was full of cops."

Bacciagaloop looked into the distance as he puffed. "And the broad ran off the two *cafones*?"

Sammy sighed. "That's what the kid said."

"Get the fuck outta here."

"The kid said he was coming back from the joint on Houston and he seen Ross fight the two big guys. It didn't go so well. The blond comes round the corner like she was shot out of a cannon and she's all Bruce fucking Lee. She's jumping and twirling and batting these mooks around like they're blowup dolls."

Bacciagaloop pushed the two strands of hair that guarded the top of his head into place. "Find out what the fuck that's about."

"He told me he's outta the subway. Investigating that Jew diamond guy who got whacked."

"The guy who was washing the Colombians' money?"

"Yeah. But according to the kid, these weren't no Colombians. They looked like they'd escaped from Fort Dix."

"Find the fuck out what the fuck that's fucking about," ordered Bacciagaloop.

"Never heard of such a thing," said Sally, "beaten up by a broad. *Marrone.*"

"And make sure the kid's all right."

"The kid? He's fine," said Sammy.

"No, not that kid. Linda's kid. I made a pledge. Nobody's killing her kid in my neighborhood," said Bacciagaloop. "Not without my say-so."

******

Ross awoke at 2 a.m. with his ribs throbbing. He would have given tender parts of his anatomy for a shot of tequila, but he had taken a Percocet and then another for good luck before calling it a night. He found his cigarettes in the dark and cracked the window so the smoke wouldn't awaken Tori. She was gorgeous, but she also scared the hell out of him.

Tori reminded Ross of Danielle D'Angelo from his teenage days. Danielle had a dark beauty – big, dark eyes; black hair that fell to her shoulders – and a pile of attitude. At 15, she was tough and she didn't take shit from anyone. He'd seen her walk into a group of kids at school and punch a boy in the face for some insult. She was breathtaking.

Ross watched the arrival of the sick and injured across the street bathed in swirling red light. This street was noisier than Candy in the sack. But she was probably lying about that, too. He didn't want her back, and that, finally, was the truth.

What an odd turn of events. He was about to eat his service revolver when he found out Candy had ripped him off. He was genuinely ready to die at the hands of a subway mugger just four nights earlier. And now, he was sprung from the underground decoy detail. He had a force of just one to reckon with: the blond vixen asleep in the next room.

He was actually looking forward to the next day.

Chapter 12

The sun was in full force, and Lyle Rucker felt perspiration bead down his spine as the man next to him, President James H. Morgan, declared National Adoption Month. Photographers roamed the Rose Garden to document the event.

Oblivious to the ceremonial words of the President, Rucker focused on the clicking of camera shutters in the seat of power. The President spoke loudly to be heard over the traffic coursing through the streets surrounding the fortification known as the White House.

"As Americans, one of our most sacred duties is to ensure that every child has a good home and the opportunity to partake in the American dream," the President said. The crowd applauded enthusiastically. On cue, a tiny black child wandered up to the President and he scooped her up and smiled energetically.

Debbie Rucker, as co-chair of the campaign that she had ingeniously named Make Adoptions More Available (MAMA), was surrounded by a gaggle of multi-hued children. The President's aides gently eased him into the picture.

The President posed for more pictures with the invited guests ("And *this* was with the *President* at the *White House*"). The ceremony was over at last.

Tom Catapano, the President's senior counselor,

tapped Rucker on the shoulder. "Hi, Tom," said Rucker. "Good to see you, buddy."

"Thanks for coming up from Houston." He shook hands and turned to Debbie. "Lovely as ever, Mrs. Rucker. Lovely dress." He took her hand gently, smiled and bowed.

"Please, Mr. Catapano, it's Debbie. I'm just a cowgirl from Texas."

"Of course you are," he replied, and the three of them laughed. "Call me Tom," he said.

"Just like in the newspapers," Debbie said. Aside from being the master strategist behind the rise of James Morgan, Catapano was the dashing man about town whom the gossip media loved to cover. A week earlier, he had had a well-chronicled evening out with the curvaceous co-star of a box-office-leading action movie. He was just "Tom" to headline writers across the nation.

"I believe the President is about to buttonhole your husband," Catapano whispered to Debbie. "I would be thrilled if I could take you to lunch in the White House mess." He smiled broadly.

"I would be delighted," she said, taking his arm.

"Lyle," the President said, "walk with me. We'll have lunch in the Oval Office Dining Room." Rucker flashed to dinners of beans and cornbread as a kid back in Laredo. His family could barely afford spit; now he was walking the corridors of the White House alongside the President. Without the small fortune in Rucker oil money that flowed to a political action group, Jim Morgan would probably still be the senior senator from Maine.

The President led Rucker to a small study where a table had been set with White House china. A steward entered and served bowls of seafood bisque.

"Lyle, I want to thank you for your service to the country," Morgan said. "This effort of ours is vital in advancing the interests and the security of the United States. I wish I could state this publicly, but of course … "

"Of course," Rucker allowed. The soup tasted of saffron and sherry, a far cry from the snapper stew his mother would make when young Lyle caught an unlucky turtle in Casa Blanca Lake. "Mr. President, if I can ever be of service to the country, you know where to find me."

"Indeed, I do," Morgan said. "And I want to assure you that because of your efforts there will be many new opportunities. Your support over the years has been invaluable to this administration, and you should know that we never forget who our friends are." The steward returned to serve poached Dover sole.

The two men talked about mutual friends and their families as they ate their lunch. The President's daughter had just started at Yale, and his son had begun working on Wall Street.

"Sir," Rucker said, "I must say that you're holding onto your youth in the White House. Seemed like Jimmy Carter was all crow's feet and gray hair once those lines formed at the gas stations." The President laughed.

"You know, Lyle," he said, "you get the best information you can get and you make the best decision you can make. Your wife will still love you. Your kids will still look up to you. And that's the key."

"Yes sir," Rucker replied. "That is the key." They chuckled. Rucker looked out the window at the greenery beyond the President. "Mr. President, thank you for granting me some time today. Pardon me for saying so, but I wanted to clear up some operating guidelines on our Venezuela endeavor." The President looked stricken.

"I … uh," Morgan stammered. The door swung open and Dennis Bouton entered at a trot.

"Excuse me, gentlemen. Mr. President, I'm sorry sir, your call to Moscow is being placed." The President swung blank-faced toward Bouton.

"Of course," he said at last. "Thank you, Dennis. I'm so, so sorry to have to run, Lyle, but the Russians await. Let's talk soon." He extended a hand and Rucker shook it glumly.

"Mr. Rucker," Bouton said, "as long as we've got you in the White House, I'd love to chat."

"Am I being taken to the woodshed?" Rucker asked, his voice rising. "You were listening in?" Bouton's jaw clenched.

"Let's think for a moment," Bouton said. "Do you suppose the President can have any knowledge of this operation? Do you know how far out of bounds all of this is? Don't you know how this works?"

"Don't you hand me that bullshit, sonny. Do you know who the fuck I am? Without me none of you are here!" Rucker was on his feet. He suddenly remembered Bouton's origins as a Marine officer.

"You can't leave bodies all over New York!" Bouton bellowed. "You're out of control. I didn't sanction cowboy assassinations in the streets of Manhattan!"

"You little weasel! You knew what this job was about!" Rucker, white hot, was not above decking this stuffed shirt right there in the White House. Three Secret Service agents entered the room to find Rucker and Bouton nose to nose.

"I'm sorry gentlemen, but we have to clear this room now," an agent said. "Mr. Rucker, we'll escort you out."

******

The Statue of Liberty loomed ahead, pointing her torch toward the Verrazano Narrows and out to sea. The October wind cut through the handful of hardy passengers determined to   make the voyage out on deck. Skip McKenzie and Ironhead Hummel had been through much, much worse.

"So this is what we fought for?" Hummel asked McKenzie.

McKenzie shook his head. "A statue made in France? I don't think so."

"It still chokes me up," said Hummel. "My great-grandfather came through Ellis Island from Germany. Hummel means bumblebee." McKenzie kept his gaze on the statue. He didn't blink. An Asian tourist with his wife and two small children approached with a camera in hand, looked at the two large men and thought better of asking them to take a picture.

"I really want to see *Phantom of the Opera*," Hummel said.

"Fine, get the tickets. I never said I wouldn't go."

Hummel watched a Coast Guard boat cross the harbor.

"I never realized there was so much water around New York."

McKenzie stared straight ahead.

"Do you ever think about what we do?" Hummel asked. "Does it ever bother you?"

"Every day," said McKenzie. Now he turned and looked at Hummel. "Do you think they ever wonder about running us out of the service? Do you think they gave half a dry fart about us? Think *they* think about *us*? Ever?"

Hummel sighed. The ferry cut through the cold water toward Liberty Island.

"I wish I'd kept my fucking mouth shut," he said at last. "Maybe I was wrong."

"You know what you saw," McKenzie snapped. "Don't start this again. Here's where we are. Deal with it."

Chapter 13

Ross studied the dreary scenery along Route 3 as he and Tori drove to Clifton, N.J., to try to connect Tony Bozzo to someone higher up the food chain. Ross drove, since Tori couldn't find Times Square with a GPS. It had been her idea to go after an associate, and the number of another former SEAL named Bill Kozloski appeared prominently in Bozzo's cell phone.

"God this is incredibly ugly," Tori pronounced as their unmarked navy blue Impala crossed a bridge over what could have been a toxic sludge pit of some sort.

"If it were pretty, then everyone would want to live here," Ross offered. He took an exit and the landscape improved, but only slightly. They passed nondescript shopping centers, doughnut shops and Polish grocery stores. Minutes later they pulled up in front of a two-story frame house in need of a new coat of yellow paint.

"I'll talk my way in," Tori said. "You slip in the back. Toss his paperwork. You've got 30 minutes and then we're out."

"Fine."

Ross stayed in the car and watched Tori, slinky in a rust-colored turtleneck and low-rise jeans, knock on the door and talk briefly to Kozloski, who looked like Hulk Hogan's ugly brother. Kozloski was buying whatever

Tori was selling. They disappeared inside, and Ross headed around to the back of the house. The backyard was surrounded by a rusty wire fence. Patrolling the scraggly yard was a brown pit bull that looked like a canine version of Kozloski. The dog spotted Ross and growled and snorted as it tore across the bare yard to the spot on its side of the fence closest Ross.

"What the fuck," he said to himself. He quickly thought of three options: shoot the dog, hop the fence and … (not much of an option at all), or create a diversion. As Ross thought and the dog drooled mad-dog drool all over itself, his cell phone rang.

"Just come around the front," Tori said.

"Huh?"

"Cement head heard the dog and saw you standing out back so I knocked him out. Come in the front."

Ross found Kozloski out cold in the living room. Tori had secured his hands behind his back with nylon cuff bands.

"What the hell is this?" Ross demanded.

"What are you talking about, genius?" said Tori, narrowing her eyes.

"You walked into the guy's house and knocked him out? No warrant, no nothin'."

Tori fixed an expression indicating she had finally found the dumbest earthling on the planet. "Look," she said, "I know you just had a head injury, but try to stick with me. This guy is a former Navy SEAL. Their specialty is death and destruction. This isn't some New York tough guy; this guy has been trained to kill by the United States Government. Your tax dollars, you know? He's connected to a guy who did a hit in a public place using a silencer. You didn't have a problem shooting that guy in the brain."

"But — "

"Shut up. I'm not through." She glared and Ross looked away. He thought of Danielle D'Angelo. "I was there. I heard Herron explain in English that this is not a police op. But maybe that's not your best language. We need to get to the bad guys before they fuck up some normal average people in your dirty little city."

Ross was silent.

"Are you good with this?" Tori asked. "I need to know now, otherwise I'll call Herron right now and tell him this is a big fucking waste of my time. Do you realize what's at stake here?"

Ross held up his hand. "Stop," he said. "Just stop. Message received. I get it."

"Good." She looked at him carefully, then turned back toward the unconscious SEAL.

She dialed Kozloski's cell phone and they found it ringing in an upstairs room with a computer and a file cabinet. She downloaded the data on his phone to a flash drive and then did the same to the C drive on his PC. Ross found several files for records from muscle-for-hire jobs. A file labeled "Strakis Solutions" contained copies of confirmation for flights to Tucson, Ariz., for Kozloski and … Tony Bozzo.

"Got something here," he called to Tori.

She looked it over and said, "Take it."

"Let's get out of here before the Hulk wakes up," he said.

"No, I want to talk to that bad boy." It was only a moment before Kozloski came back to life.

"My fucking head. What did you do to me? Take these fucking cuffs off!" he roared.

"Hey, Billy, got any ice tea?" Ross said. "Maybe *Arizona* Ice Tea. I'll bet you drink a lot of that." Kozloski rolled over onto his side to get a better look at Ross.

"Who the fuck are you?"

"He's the guy who shot Tony Bozzo," said Tori, tossing her blond hair out of her blue eyes. Kozloski looked back at Ross and studied him closer.

"Tony got shot?" he said to Tori. Then, to Ross: "What are you, FBI?" Ross gave a tiny you-figure-it-out nod.

"Yeah. I knew someone who looked like her wouldn't be taking a survey. But darling, I give free mustache rides."

"I was thinking of taking those cuffs off," she said, "but if you're going to talk trash, *William*, I have a mini set here" she fished around in her pocket, "that ought to fit your balls."

"OK, OK, I'll behave. Just ask your questions and leave me alone." Tori freed him and he sat rubbing his wrists in an easy chair that Archie Bunker might have thrown out in the early '70s.

"Did I run into you a couple days ago in SoHo?" Ross asked.

"No. I never saw you until you broke into my house."

"Bill," Tori said, "tell me about Strakis. What were you and Tony doing in Tucson?" Kozloski looked hard at Tori, then at a stain on the exhausted carpet. Ross figured the pit bull had put the spot there.

"Look." He exhaled a long breath. "We were in Afghanistan together, me and Boz. It was tough there. He got wounded twice, me once. One time I got grabbed by some Taliban in the middle of a firefight. Just got separated and I'm surrounded by these mooks, and here comes Boz. Smoked 'em all and got me back on the right side.

"Anyway, you come out of that, back here, and it's not the same. I'm a SEAL; I've got a lot of training. I can overrun an enemy position, or handle underwater demolition, or fast-rope out of a helicopter. But what does that give you when you come home? You know how hard it is for an ex-SEAL to get a regular job? No one wants to touch us. They're afraid of us."

"Tucson, Bill," Tori said. "What did you do in Tucson?"

"These people come at you because of your training. They have black bag jobs. Muscle jobs, maybe a little burglary. They're loons, but the pay is great. A couple of those a year and you can live in splendor." He waved at the splendor of his current surroundings. "I never felt comfortable doing those. But Boz would take anything, and he got me in on Strakis."

"What was the job?" Ross asked.

Kozloski sighed. "Some guy hooked in with the Colombians. Boz knew him." Tori and Ross exchanged a look.

"And?" Tori prodded.

"Diamonds. We stole some diamonds."

******

Alex Cordero wasn't going to get his hopes up. He'd had two hearings before the parole board and been rejected. After 23 years behind prison walls, he knew, even if something in his gut told him he had a chance, he was best to believe he had none.

"What you got, Irv?" he asked his cellmate. Irv sat on the lower bunk reading a letter. The lower had been Cordero's bunk, but he'd switched when Irv began to have difficulty climbing up to the higher bunk as he hit his mid-fifties.

"Another one of those letters. I don't understand it. A woman from Levittown. Wants to be my friend." He looked up. "A total stranger."

"You're still famous, Irv."

Irv Kaplan had hired a hitman to break into his Westchester County home and shoot his wife. Irv had a 26-year-old girlfriend whom he thought he could keep a secret from investigators. He owned three restaurants and was planning to live the sweet life with a young wife in place of the aging, original model. It was a stupid plan – one of the oldest motives in civilization – and investigators never looked at anyone but Irv.

Irv crumbled the letter and threw it into the trash can next to the toilet. "Fuck that," he said. "What am I gonna do when they spring you, Alex?"

"Irv, please. Don't even say it. I'm only getting out of here in a box."

"Bullshit."

"For real. I killed a man. His son's a cop. Blue sticks with blue."

Irv shook his head emphatically. "But you're no criminal anymore. You could *help* on the outside. You won't be another unemployed con."

"Ain't gonna happen, Irv."

"Let's just say it did. What am I gonna do? You saved my life twice. They respect you."

"Look, it ain't gonna happen, Irv. But just to be sure, I'll talk to the crews. I'll tell them they shouldn't mess with you."

"I'd appreciate it, Alex. I'm not sure why I care so much about staying alive in here, but I'm not ready to pack it in just yet."

Chapter 14

Tom Catapano watched as his Secret Service detachment led the town car up the drive of Raf Oliva's Key Biscayne house.

Vanessa Lamond popped from the back of the car and rushed into Catapano's arms. "God, I missed you," she said and gave the President's counselor a soft, passionate kiss.

"You look absolutely breathtaking," he said. She wore a silk top over designer jeans. Her shoes seemed all heel, with just a strand or two of leather to keep them on her feet. With the extra lift, she saw eye to eye with the six-foot Catapano. Her brown hair was pinned up.

"Not exactly a movie star outfit, but I don't think anyone recognized me." She took off her sunglasses.

"Now there's the face that America loves," he said. He kissed her again. "You'd look ravishing in a burlap sack."

She nuzzled him and purred in his ear, "I could devour you."

"That is encouraged, love." He smiled boyishly and slipped an arm around her. "Come in out of the driveway. This place is really fantastic. I hope you like it."

He led her through the house to the terraced pool area, overlooking Biscayne Bay.

"Oh, Tom, this is so beautiful!" she cooed.

"*You're* so beautiful, Vaness. This is picturesque."

A few wispy clouds dotted the azure sky. Vanessa scanned the bay from one turquoise end to another. She reached back to unfasten a clip and let her hair fall around her shoulders.

"You're right, Tom. This is *amazing.*"

"Let's get a drink, and I'll show you the rest."

"Just make mine Pellegrino with lime. I have to start shooting in 10 days. They're paying me $21 million, so the least I can do is try to keep the cellulite off my ass. There's a lot of skin in the script."

"Let me be the judge of your ass."

She threw her head back and laughed heartily. Catapano loved actresses, not just for their beauty and glamour but for their outsized emotions and outspokenness. Monthly trysts with Vanessa Lamond were all peaks and no valleys. He didn't think he could bear having her more frequently than that.

They headed into the house. She was enraptured by the round kitchen, with teak cabinets and circular island counter. "I'm doing this in my Malibu house," she announced. "I adore this kitchen. Remind me to take pictures."

They reached the master bedroom at last. She put her drink down and peeled off her blouse and jeans. "That feels good," she said. "Let me freshen up."

"I don't want you fresh," he said. "I prefer you dirty."

She smiled. "You evil man." She reached around to unhook her bra. "As you wish." She removed her panties and lay down on the massive bed. She spread her legs wide and smiled a big-screen smile. "A pungent woman, for your dirty pleasures."

Catapano's wide grin evaporated as his phone began to buzz.

"Is it him?"

He checked his phone. "It's him. I have to use the

encrypted phone," he said with anguish. "The only person in the world who could make me walk away from … " he gestured at the most intimate part of her voluptuous body.

Vanessa erupted in hysterics. "You should see your face!" She doubled over. She had a throaty, convulsive laugh that those around her usually found to be infectious. "Go, go. Attend to the country. Tell the President he's keeping a naked woman waiting. I'll keep my motor running."

******

Catapano slipped back to the bedroom 20 minutes later to find her asleep exactly where he'd left her. He stripped off his shirt and pants and began to gently massage her feet. She moaned softly. Her eyes were closed, but a smile crept across her mouth.

He worked her toes and the tops of her feet, then the pressure points on her soles. She was no longer asleep, but her eyes remained shut. "That's amaaaazing," she sighed. "Talented at politics *and* massage. It's not fair."

He had not yet worked his way above her ankles. "You ain't seen nothing yet," he replied. He spent 10 minutes on her calves and behind her knees, working patiently up to her thighs, with forays to her buttocks. He slid up to her lower back, tracing the length of her spine to her neck and shoulders. His efforts were answered with ecstatic moans and grunts. The lapping of Biscayne Bay and the rustling of the palms on the terrace provided an ethereal soundtrack.

He finished at the base of her head and kissed her exposed cheek. She grabbed hold of him and wrestled him onto his back. The woman who commanded more than $20 million per role liked to be on top. Here we are, Catapano thought with amusement, at the juncture of politics and popular culture.

At last, they collapsed in a sweaty embrace, their

chests heaving in unison.

"Did anyone ever tell you that you were skilled at seduction?" Vanessa asked.

"I've built my career around it," Catapano said.

"Hmmm," she said, "something else we have in common."

Later, he showed her the wonder that was the master bath. They showered in a cavernous transparent enclosure on the bayside corner of the house. The effect was as if they were suspended over the water. He kneaded her shoulders and neck as the hot water flowed over their bodies.

"How am I going to sneak you onto the set?" she said.

"Just doing my part for the arts."

"I thought I was doing *my* part for the nation."

They dressed in robes and watched the light fade over the bay. He persuaded her to have a mojito, arguing that the caloric intake was equal to what they had expended with their lovemaking.

"To success," he toasted. "May we make good use of it while it lasts."

"Amen to that," she said. They clinked glasses and drank.

******

Dennis Bouton labored on. He'd split the day between the State Department and Langley, trying to formulate options on Somalia. It was 9:30, past the kids' bedtime, not that they realized fathers sometimes were home to read a story and tuck them in.

Bouton recalled the Thanksgiving when young Mandee had come home from school with a third-grade assignment. The teacher had given the class sheets of paper with sentences that had a word missing. They were to fill in the noun.

On Thanksgiving, I will eat turkey, said one

sentence.

On Thanksgiving, I will visit <u>Grandma</u>, said another.

On Thanksgiving, I will see <u>Dad</u>, was how Mandee had filled in another sentence.

Not surprisingly, State and the Agency agreed on little. All the better to build an analysis of wide-ranging possibilities.

What worried him was his flagging endurance. He shouldn't be held to anything short of Marine standards because he now wore civilian clothes and worked in an office. But he found it difficult to sleep. His stomach was troubling him. And Mary – when he saw her at all – was becoming distant and impatient. She'd suffered through his deployments throughout his military career and expected something more close to normal in Washington.

Some small part of him wanted to chuck it and find a well-paying job among the growing ranks of private security contractors. Sell the tract house in Falls Church and move in next to Raf on Biscayne Bay. But those people struck him as profiteers and mercenaries, out to score regardless of the effects on the country. He could never explain that sort of work to Jesus.

So for him, there really was no option. Soldiers didn't quit on the battlefield. He'd press on, until the final days of the administration. And then … who knew?

He'd have to get to Catapano quickly to dampen any fallout over the Rucker incident with the President. After all, the President's senior counselor had been the one to suggest that the Venezuelan op be outsourced to Rucker. He should have known how erratic the guy was. And his man North struck him more and more as being a smug Boy Scout who was a few merit badges short of a sash.

When the stuff hit the fan, it would be Dennis Bouton sitting before a Congressional inquiry, not the cowboys from Texas.

Bouton turned to the plate of General Tso's

Chicken his secretary had fetched for dinner. It was a collage of congealed grease. He swung his desk light lower and returned to the Somalia options.

Chapter 15

Herron arranged for Ross and Tori to fly West on a small government jet with the proviso that they were not to talk to anyone who happened to be riding along. Tori wore her hair up and tucked under a baseball cap that said "BFD" on the front.

"BFD? Boston Fire Department," Ross asked.

"BFD: Big fucking deal," she answered.

Shortly before takeoff, three refrigerator-sized young men boarded, took seats in the back, donned headphones and went to sleep. The plane touched down in Dallas to drop them off.

Ross had never been west of Chicago, so he was mesmerized by the terrain below: sun-dried earth; long, ruler-straight country roads; snow-topped ranges and peaks. The plane finally crossed into the valley where Tucson sprawled to fill in the desert between four mountain ranges.

Minutes later, Ross, Tori and the crew were stepping across the airfield. The sun had a ferocity Ross had never experienced, even though a stiff wind kept the heat moderate. The air was dry and pure. It seemed to *taste* fresh to Ross, who had had a steady diet of burned asbestos brake linings, mold, urine and rodent feces for two years in the subway. They checked into a nondescript dreary motel near the nondescript dreary downtown.

Promising the best tacos he'd ever had, Tori took Ross to a little tacqueria in South Tucson, the nearly completely Mexican end of town. She procured from the counter two plates brimming with tacos.

"What is this?" Ross asked.

"Just eat it; you'll like it."

Ross dug in and did, indeed, like it. This was nothing like the generally lousy Mexican food in New York. He found it astonishing that, in a city where you could have Afghan kabobs delivered to your door in the middle of the night, authentic Mexican food was as rare as a native-born taxi driver.

His hands were wet with the pungent runoff of the tacos. "That was good. What did I just eat?"

"One was lengua. Tongue."

"OK, like the deli. That's cool, I like tongue. You gave me tongue. Awesome."

"Shut up." Tori shook her head dismissively.

"Another was carne asada. Kind of a stringy meat that's marinated for a long time and grilled."

"Steak sandwich on a taco."

"And the third one was cabeza."

That sounded familiar. Ross scanned his high school Spanish.

"Cabeza. Head? I ate a head?"

"Well, more like cheek. Goat cheek."

Ross made a sour face. "Can I pick the next restaurant?"

"No."

"That doesn't seem fair."

"Who said anything was fair? You know nothing about Tucson, and even less about food."

"How do you come to know so much about Tucson?"

"I've done a lot of work down here. There's a huge Air Force base. A ton of military contractors. They make a lot of missiles. They even have some old nuclear missile silos. They were ready to fire until they were deactivated after the SALT Treaty. There's a lot of espionage. It's also a big way station for smugglers. Always has been."

"Do they have anything to eat here besides Mexican?"

"Yes. There's a great Guatemalan restaurant."

They drove to the address they had for the offices of Strakis Solutions. The town was a little beat up, but Ross liked that cactus popped up even in developed commercial areas. This was not a Sun Belt city rolled out over the desert; the desert was still here. And there. Ross felt the opposite of claustrophobia.

The address turned out to be a self-storage complex.

The analysts from the Intelligence Division had put together a terse report gleaned from scraps of data from databases that average people would be frightened to know existed. The analysts could find someone's third cousin if they lived part of the year on the dark side of the moon. They had discovered that Strakis Solutions was operated by George Rivera, 52, born in Agua Prieta, Sonora, just over the border in Mexico. One of the biggest businesses in Agua Prieta was digging tunnels under the border fence. He also owned a bar called the Agave Lounge and a used car lot called Freddy's Discount Cars. Local intelligence had indicated he was a bit of a matchmaker for elements of the Mexican underworld. Ross got the impression of a Latino Sammy Napolitano.

"I think I know how to play this," Ross told Tori. "Let's go to the bar."

"Have you ever gone an hour without a drink?"

"Yeah, once, I think. Can you go an hour without busting my balls?"

"You didn't complain when I stopped those guys from jumping up and down on them."

He wasn't sure how he felt about Tori since she had lectured him in Kozloski's living room. But she certainly was wonderful to look at.

"My balls thank you," he said in a humble manner. Ross looked at the map. "Now we're up here north, seems like to best way to the bar is — "

"Don't worry about it; I know this town. Besides, you don't need a map if you can read the mountains. Those are the Catalinas right there. They're north." She gave him that narrowed-eye look that he was coming to know as trouble. "But aren't you forgetting something?"

"Please? Thank you?"

"No, dumb ass. We're already here. He's got a locker in there somewhere that might have something of interest in it."

"Fine. How do you propose we get into it? You know: big fat locks, metal gates."

Tori looked at the storage center office, across a scratchy thicket of cactus needles and snake holes from where they sat in the car. She pulled binoculars from the glove compartment. "Perfect." She pulled a small bag from the trunk. "There's a guy about your age in the office all by himself. Figure he's pulling down – oh, eight bucks an hour to sit there and be bored shitless. I'm going to distract him. I guarantee he'll be out of that office and you can find the locker and the pass key."

"He's just going to up and leave," Ross said skeptically.

"Do you want to get a warrant?" She flashed the how-can-anyone-be-dumber-than-you look. "I guarantee that guy will bolt from that office."

Tori nodded toward the office. "Head around back and wait for him to come out. Go this way, but don't step on any rattlers."

"Snakes?"

Every step seemed booby-trapped with some kind of shrub that held needles or teeth or that maybe concealed a snake or God knows what else was out here to kill you, or at least make you really miserable. As he made a wide arc out of view of the office, he heard the car pull closer to the building.

Ross was two-thirds of the way to the office when a man popped outside as if he were spring loaded. He was looking intently toward the car. Ross turned to look, too. Tori was doing a strip tease. She took off the ball cap and shook out her golden hair. She leaned into the backseat in a way to afford storage-clerk guy a VIP-lounge glimpse of her ass. Ross needed every ounce of will to keep moving.

Within 30 seconds, Ross had found a clipboard holding a list cross-referencing storage units with renters. He found the key seconds later. He texted Tori ("301G"), who appeared to be down to bra and panties. Ross wished his vision were better.

By the time Ross found the locker, Tori was already standing in front of it. She was wearing an orange T-shirt and cut-off jeans and looking like she had just modeled the new Daisy Mae line at Fashion Week. The locker was about the size of Leslie's house of tattoos apartment in Alphabet City. Inside, the perimeter was filled with burlap-wrapped bales piled to the ceiling. Weed. A ton or more, Ross estimated. In a space at the rear were two footlockers. They were unlocked. Tori popped one open: M4 carbines.

"Big surprise," Ross said.

"Let's get out of here," Tori answered.

******

The Agave Lounge – the *World Famous* Agave Lounge, the sign said – was a dive bar in a quiet section of Tucson just north of the undistinguished downtown. The city's skyline consisted of three tall office buildings that would have been dwarves in New York. Ross encouraged Tori to give George Rivera's house a toss while Ross worked the bar, but she still considered him a loser who would surely be murdered if she left him out of her sight for too long. She would "monitor" from the parking lot; they both feared a riot would ensue if she were to walk unaccompanied into the place. He would come outside for a smoke on the quarter-hour; if he didn't show, Tori would come looking for him.

Ross sat at the bar and ordered a beer. They had Rolling Rock. At a little past 4 in the afternoon, there were two Latino men wearing straw cowboy hats shooting pool and a sprinkling of other men who looked more like elderly alcoholics than desperados. The bartender was a small, slender young woman wearing a tank top that displayed barbed wire tattoos on each biceps and some modest artwork on the back of each shoulder. Her name, it turned out, was Lenny, which stood for nothing; that's what her parents had named her.

"Were you named after Lenny Bruce?"

"Who?

"Lenny Dykstra?"

"Who?"

"Lenny Kravitz?"

"You're silly."

Ross made more trips to the men's room than were necessary after two beers, each time venturing farther out of bounds, trying closed doors here and there, searching for Rivera's office. He figured he'd found it when he finally came to a locked door that seemed to lead to a large space in a corner of the building. He could hear no voices or movement inside.

The bar room was dark and dusty. And yet, these were happy drunks – hopeless and penniless but apparently living their dream.

Outside for an I'm-not-dead smoke, Ross saw a yellow Hummer turn into the parking lot and head around to the back. He caught Tori's eye and eye-pointed at the Hummer. Ross crept around the corner and saw two men – one gray-haired and portly, the other younger and fit – enter a back door.

Ross slipped back inside. A band had begun to set up on a small stage on the other side of the two pool tables. He re-parked on his bar stool and glimpsed Rivera and his henchman come out of the back and talk to the band members. Handshakes, backslaps, laughter. Rivera came to the bar and hailed Lenny. They conferred for a minute, and Rivera and his boy went back to the office. Ross signaled for a refill. The Rolling Rock cost half as much as at Flynn's. Was Manhattan real estate that expensive?

"That guy looked important," Ross told Lenny, gesturing to where the boss had huddled with her a half-minute ago.

"Owns the place," Lenny said. She chewed gum as she sponged up the bar. Flirty, even without eye contact. Ross began to wonder about his prospects with the slightly tattooed bartendress if the encounter with Rivera didn't run completely off the rails. Petite women, he had come to find, had acrobatic talents lacking in the more fulsome.

"That George?"

"Yep," Lenny said. "Nice guy. You know him?"

"Friend of a friend. I should say hello."

"He's just in the back there. Turn right, last door on the left. Just give a knock." She winked. Why did he like these tattooed bad girls? For one, they were found in bars.

"Thanks, Lenny. Has anyone told you recently how cute you are?"

"Yeah." She giggled. "My husband."

As Ross finished his beer he thought about the DeSimone case. Trying to get a break in his investigation, he'd gone to the bar of a mobster on Franklin Street. The guy instantly made him for a cop, guns were drawn, the backups crashed in. No, he'd need to take it slower.

He had 30 minutes to his next smoke signal.

Chapter 16

Lyle Rucker's anger seemed to dissipate with every mile he put between Washington and his Gulfstream G500. He sipped an Australian shiraz and tapped idly on his laptop, reading his analysts' latest report on the Maracaibo Basin, Venezuela's leading oil gusher. Rucker wanted a well there like he had wanted the sexiest cheerleader in Dallas. The richer and more successful he got, the juicier the opportunities that were handed to him. But was this one slipping away?

Rucker began to boil again when he thought about the millions he'd heaped on the campaigns of the pansy in the White House. Boys, pretending to do a man's job. He'd settle the score with Bouton, the no-nuts flunky. If there was one thing Rucker learned in his climb up in the world, it was that you never let someone get away with crossing you, no matter how long it took to get even. The waiting was *not* the hardest part; it was something to savor.

He was beginning to wonder about Matt North. He'd put the Venezuelan operation together smoothly, but then made an amateurish mistake. He'd trusted the Colombians and they'd duped him and there was nothing they could do about it. He was smooth, but there was also a slickness that made Rucker uneasy. He'd taken some precautions with North because Rucker didn't believe in risks. Even the Lord pulled a fast one on you now and again.

There were always options. Rucker could talk the hide off a cow; he could make them Washington boys come around. He could deliver twice the results they were expecting. Once they had Gallegos and his banditos on the ropes, he'd take it from there. He could work with the South Americans.

Work with the South Americans.

Maybe there was another way. Something more elegant than the convoluted plan the White House had brought them on for. And then that little pissant Bouton would get his.

******

Ross knocked authoritatively three times.

Rivera's office fit with the rest of the bar in the same way that blond, beautiful Marilyn fit with the rest of the Munsters. The paneling was mahogany. Prints of Geronimo and fellow warriors, circa 1880, hung on a wall. Ross guessed the sculpture was Aztec. One piece looked familiar, though Ross could not place it.

"George Rivera?"

"You got him, my friend. What can I do for you?"

Rivera was gray haired but he hadn't gone to seed. He had square shoulders and a strong chest.

Ross checked the younger man, who was inspecting Ross head to toe. He looked Apache, with high cheekbones and dark eyes that held all the sparkle of a moonless night. He wasn't so young, on closer inspection – about 45 and solid, with the face of a stone killer. Ross guessed the man hadn't smiled since LBJ lived in the White House. Still, Ross gauged the prospect of gunplay to be low.

"I'm visiting from New York and a friend said I should come by to say hello," said Ross, thinking it was an appropriately bullshit opener.

Rivera smiled. "Always happy to meet a friendly person. What's your name, buddy?"

"Ross. Ross Walton."

"Glad to meet you, Ross. This here is Mateo." Mateo looked Ross' way. That was as much of a greeting as he'd get.

"What line of work are you in, Ross?" Rivera asked.

"Diamonds mostly. Gems."

"I see. That's a big business around here. You should be here for the gem show. It's huge."

"Yeah, I should. It's my first time in town."

"And who is this friend we have in common?" Rivera asked.

"Tony Bozzo."

"Tony Bozzo. How is Tony?"

"Tony's great. You know, doing well."

Rivera's eyes went wide. He turned to look at his partner, whose expression was as unchanged as a cadaver's. "Really?" Rivera said. "I heard he was dead. I heard you shot him."

******

"How many times have you seen this movie, Ernesto?" Ruben asked.

"Probably seven, eight," Ernesto replied. "Snake Plisskin, he is the best."

"I like the title," said Roberto. "I would like to escape from New York myself.

"And do what," asked Ernesto, "be nobody, with no money in Cali?"

"It's too cold here," said Roberto. "The white people treat you like shit. The black people treat you worse."

"Start the movie, Ernesto," Ruben said, "in an hour Alvaro will deliver another load that we have to step on by morning." Ernesto hit the play button. They were so close to La Guardia that the apartment would shake when a plane took off, which was often.

About an hour later, as Ernest Borgnine tried to persuade Snake to be sensible in a New York populated by lunatics, Alvaro buzzed from the lobby. One of his two companions held the lobby door for a small boy, who lingered behind while the three Colombians made for the elevator.

Alvaro dropped the load of cocaine on the table in the kitchen. He and his companions sat down with the men to watch the movie.

"I've seen this," said Carlos. "Snake Plisskin is a badass."

As Snake fought a fearsome post-Apocalyptic bald man, the door to the apartment burst open, splinters of the door frame flying like darts.

"On the ground, *maricones!*" yelled a man wearing a ski mask and carrying a Tec-9. Three more men entered, each similarly attired and equipped. The six Colombians lay prone. One of the intruders secured their hands behind their backs with plastic cuffs.

"Do you know who we are?" Alvaro asked.

"Yeah," said the first intruder, "We know who you are." He fired a single shot into the base of Alvaro's head. "We know who you *were*." He made his way around the room, firing five more shots.

******

Ross had anticipated that Kozloski would have warned Rivera. So much for foreplay.

"The papers must be pretty good out here," Ross said. Where had he seen that Aztec figure?

"You're a funny man. That's good. I like funny people. Do you know any good jokes, Detective?"

"As a matter of fact, when I flew out here, an old man in front of me at the ticket counter tried to check three bags. He said he wanted to send one bag to

Cleveland, one to Chicago and one to LA. The woman behind the counter said they couldn't do that. 'Why not,' the old man asked, 'you did it last week.' "

"That's a cute one," Rivera said. "What do you think, Mateo?"

"It's OK," his henchman said. Ross wondered exactly where this was going. He had another 20 minutes before he would miss his next smoke break.

"Detective, I will answer your question even before you ask it: I had nothing to do with the shooting in the New York subway that you are investigating."

"And that's it?" Ross said. "I take your word for it and go home? It don't work that way where I come from." Now he had it: The Aztec design looked a lot like the tattoo on Lenny's left shoulder.

"No? How does it work?"

"I'm up your ass like a rectal itch until I find what connects you to the hit on the diamond dealer. Cause I know you like diamonds. And you'd better hope I put you somewhere safe, cause when you whacked the jeweler, you fucked up a mighty nice thing for a Colombian cartel. And they *don't* like funny people."

Rivera exchanged looks with Mateo.

"The two mercs did do a job for me, but it's not as you think. Someone stole diamonds from me, and they got them back. In my line of work, I operate in commodities much of the time and no cash, as you can understand."

"Sure," said Ross, "like monster bales of pot and M4 carbines?" Rivera and Mateo exchanged distressed looks. In his peripheral vision, Ross could see Mateo jump to his feet. Ross pulled his gun and lunged toward Rivera, holding his Beretta an inch from Rivera's face.

Looking at Rivera, Ross told Mateo, who held the muzzle of a gun to the back of Ross' head, "I'll put a bullet in his fucking eye. Think that through, smart guy." Ross stared at Rivera, whose expression had not changed. Rivera stared past Ross at Mateo.

"You get credit for being the big hero," Ross told Mateo. He felt the muzzle of Mateo's gun withdraw from a spot above his right ear. "Are we done now?" Ross asked. They put the guns away.

"Detective Walton, I will leave you with one bit of advice before you leave here. In the Southwest, size does not impress us. In our desert lives the scorpion. The larger scorpions are to be avoided, but it is the smaller ones that have the most poisonous sting."

Ross got up to go. "I have no fucking idea what you're talking about."

Chapter 17

Tori and Ross stood on a lonely patch of desert west of town, not far from where Hollywood had worked to keep America plied with Westerns for decades.

"The idea here is to not get hit," said Tori. "If you don't get hit, you don't wind up in Bellevue."

"I knew that," said Ross.

She circled to Ross' left and snapped a kick that connected with his thigh. "You didn't say anything about kicking," he said, grimacing.

She stood still. "All right, you hit *me*."

Ross circled to his left and snapped a left jab. It cruised by harmlessly as Tori leaned to her right. She grabbed hold of his straightened left arm with both hands and brought him to his knees with an arm bar that threatened to bend a joint in a direction it normally would not turn.

"OK OK OK!" he said. "I get your point. Can you show me that *slower*? Please?"

She stared at him but wouldn't release his arm.

"Read and react," she said.

"Arm." He looked down at the trapped arm and back at her.

"Balance," she said.

"I'll do better, I swear," he said, wincing, "give me my fucking arm back. Please, killer blond lady."

Tori dropped his arm and stood back to study his T-shirt, which said, in tiny lettering, "I'm With Smarty."

"I know, I know," he said. "That makes me Stupid."

She formed a frowny smile. "I don't think I've ever met anyone like you."

******

Linda Walton dared not cry. She had managed to keep the parole hearing a secret from Ross. Now she wished he were here. Not to look at the man who had killed his father, but to help steady her. She had to speak. But first, yet another corrections official explained how the man who had murdered her husband was the model of rehabilitation, a positive influence for fellow inmates, a stabilizing force in the prison – a saint.

"He had a significant crack cocaine addiction when he entered prison," the official said. "He entered detox and has been drug free ever since. That was 23 years ago. Now he counsels other inmates. During his two decades of incarceration he has embraced education, earned his high school diploma and a college degree and is working on his dissertation for a master's in social work. I'd describe Alex Cordero as the gold standard for the rehabilitated prisoner."

The official was excused, and they called Linda down to the seat in front of the board members.

"Mrs. Walton, we'd like to hear from you as part of this review."

She cleared her throat and looked at the words she had prepared. She folded the paper twice and kept it in her hand. Be polite when addressing the board, the information sheet had stressed.

"Ladies and gentlemen of the board, I'm speaking on behalf of my husband, Doug Walton, the victim. I've heard a lot about how much Mr." – she hesitated to say his name – "Cordero has done with his life in prison." She looked over at him and their eyes met briefly before he looked down. She felt as if the breath had gone out of her.

"It's commendable" she said, "it really is." It was no use; the tears began to flow. "But my husband can't come home after 23 years. My two sons grew up without a father. He killed one man and changed three other people's lives forever. None of us can come home." She shook her head to indicate that she couldn't go on.

"Thank you, Mrs. Walton," the chairman said.

******

Ross made Tori repeat the ground rules.

"You heard me: If you can beat me, you can have me."

"Define *have*."

"It's not gonna happen, so you don't really have to worry about it," Tori said. "I just thought you needed some encouragement."

"Well that would be very encouraging. I'd be encouraged to go for a black belt."

"You wouldn't live that long," she motioned for them to walk. "Just remember what I told you about lethal strike points."

Tori headed down a trail flanked by towering Saguaro cactuses that looked like goal posts zipped up in green corduroy jumpsuits. Ahead was a craggy mountain range. In the foreground lay a tangle of mesquite, stumpy barrel cactus, green palo verde and scraggly shrubs that seemed to have barbed wire for leaves. Even more picturesque were Tori's long legs and firm posterior, exquisitely housed in the shorts she had changed into the day before for the benefit of the self-storage clerk.

Ross took two long strides and put his hands around Tori's neck, intending to take her to the ground and …

Tori squatted down, then popped up shooting her right arm under Ross' two arms. She stepped in tight with her left leg and slammed two quick body shots off Ross' ribs, still tender from his beatdown on Jersey Street. It seemed as if she were about to rip both arms off at the shoulders.

"Ahhhh! What's the safe word?" Tori released him, and Ross sank to his knees. "OK," Ross said, his ribs searing, "you beat me, you can have me."

They climbed to a mesa with a panoramic view of downtown Tucson (such as it was) and sparred. Tori ducked, weaved and spun as Ross jabbed, hooked and crossed into thin air. As he moved in to wrestle, she kicked. He retreated. He threw a straight right that she ducked; she spun and landed a roundhouse in the neighborhood of his right temple. Hitting the ground, Ross' body made a sound like an anvil falling from a helicopter.

"Oh shit," Tori said. "Sorry, sorry, sorry." She dropped to her knees to examine him. Ross' eyes were closed; he was breathing in gasps.

"Lethal strike point. Lethal strike point," he murmured. She bent down for a closer look and Ross caught her around the shoulders, pulled her down and kissed her.

******

There was little else to do in Tucson but enjoy the weather and the ambience until an early morning clandestine commuter flight back to New York. They had established that George Rivera was as he seemed: a little scorpion trading plundered GI weapons for Mexican pot. Tori had encouraged Ross to stay for a nightcap at the World Famous Agave Lounge while she tossed Rivera's house. He guzzled Don Julio anejo tequila chased with Rolling Rock while he tried to close the deal with Lenny. She was, in fact, married – to Rivera, El Scorpionito himself.

Tori had managed to find an e-mail exchange

between Rivera and Bozzo that indicated the diamond job was a one-off (though Bozzo made a desperate pitch for more work in the Southwest or Mexico).

Tori and Ross put on their best clothes and dined at an elegant Mexican restaurant in a historic house near downtown. The evening was warm, but not hot – no humidity, no mosquitoes, no taxis honking or sirens blaring – perfect. They took a table in the courtyard, near a hanging contraption in which the chefs cured meat in the dry sun.

"Are you sore?" Tori asked. She looked radiant, reflections from the candles dancing in her eyes. Ross felt debonair in a black dress shirt and black pants. He had a prominent bruise on the side of his face from where Tori had connected with the kick.

"I'm pretty banged up." Ross laughed. "But I've never had so much fun getting my ass kicked." He flashed to his previous life, which would have had him dragging around the subway with his three non-backups at this time of night.

"A lot of experience having your ass kicked?" Tori asked.

Ross laughed. "You know, sometimes it doesn't work out so well. I usually give away a lot of weight."

"Everyone's pudgy these days. But you look," Tori shrugged her shoulders, "good."

"Hmm," said Ross.

Tori ordered for them: tamales, burritos, enchiladas. They sampled from each of the plates; she fed him random morsels with her fingers. The waiter brought more margaritas.

"This reminds me of when I was a kid," said Ross. "You run around all day and at night you feel a nice kind of tired. Like you burned off a lot of energy."

"Endorphins. You produce them during strenuous exercise. They give you a sense of well-being."

"Yeah, I know, but I read somewhere that we're happiest when we do things that take us back to childhood. That pure joy of being a kid."

Tori nodded. "Sometimes I smell something that makes me think of ski trips with my family. Pine trees. Fresh snow. Hot chocolate."

"The sea," Ross said. "Fishing with my dad on boats out of Brooklyn. I love that sea smell." Tori stiffened at the mention of Ross' dad. She had read the bio Herron had prepared when he brought her in.

"I like the beach. But I burn," Tori said.

"And funnel cake."

"Ew."

"Yeah, but only because it reminds me of the San Gennaro festival. We'd wander all over and have a ball as kids."

"I had funnel cake at the Jefferson County Fair. Gave me a horrible stomach ache. We called it the 'funnel cake stomach ache.'"

Ross raised his glass.

"To William Herron," Ross toasted.

"Absolutely, to Bill Herron."

"To Billy Boy," Ross said, and they giggled and drank.

"To John Gaffney," Tori said.

"To John – who?"

"The guy who hounded me out of the Agency."

"To John the scumbag then," Ross said. They clinked and gulped their drinks.

"To — " Ross raised his glass but realized whom he was toasting.

"What?" Tori asked. "What's the matter."

Ross felt the wonder of the night drain in an instant.

"Tell me," Tori said softly.

"Eddie Ferguson," he spoke slowly. "I was thinking about the people who made this night – here with you – possible. Eddie Ferguson. I was riding the subway home one day in plainclothes. This was when I was Detective Golden Boy." Ross paused to corral his emotions. "The train stops at 14th Street – not my stop. But there's some commotion, people running around, women screaming. I pulled my piece and saw a guy running toward me on the platform. He raised his gun. I got him first. Through the chest and out the back. Through his spine. He was an undercover." The next part came slowly. Ross couldn't recall ever telling this story. "Now he's a quadriplegic."

Tori put her hand to her mouth. "You didn't know. How could you have known?"

"It was a long investigation, but yeah, that's what they said. But the other 36,000 cops on the force didn't buy it." Ross studied the meat cage. Who hangs meat in the sky? His throat seemed to swell, to contain the words. "I'm the asshole who paralyzed a cop. The guy has two little kids."

Ross continued. "I went to his room. I wanted to … " Ross struggled for the right words, "I don't know, say something. Make it right. His wife was there. She spit in my face."

Tori reached over and held Ross' hands. "Look at me. Look at me now. That's long past us. You can't look back." She half rose, leaned over the enchiladas and kissed him softly on the mouth.

They sat staring at each other until the waiter approached and asked if they would like dessert.

"Now I have a story for you," Tori said at last. She looked into her margarita as she formed what she was about to say. "I was on a job like this, partnered up with a Treasury agent. This was four years ago when I first went freelance. We were after some counterfeiters." She began to rock gently. "He – my partner – was very smart. Not so tough." She smiled at Ross to make the comparison. "He didn't even think he was tough. But he was clever and handsome and he … " she took a breath, "made me laugh."

"Well, late in the investigation, he got snatched from right under my nose." She narrowed her eyes as she continued in a monotone. "They made him suffer. They dumped his body in a busy park so we'd find it." Ross reached out and she took his hand and squeezed.

"I'm so sorry."

She smiled bravely. "Yeah, well, I made them pay."

They drove back to the motel in silence. Ross was even more disoriented in the dark in this strange city. Somewhere Lenny was pouring shots and beers for happy barflies. As Tori turned the rental car into the parking lot, Ross felt the heaviness of a question that needed to be posed exactly right, or not at all.

They parked and walked slowly to their rooms. Ross ached for a cigarette but was certain that was exactly the wrong thing to do. He opened his mouth to speak but nothing sounded appropriate. Finally they were in front of his room, next door to hers, and he stopped and looked at her, silently urgent.

She hooked his arm with hers. "Come with me," she said.

Chapter 18

Matt North felt eyes on him as he walked into the Oak Room. He wore a double-breasted suit that accentuated his broad shoulders and trim waist. Beautiful women seated next to powerful, wealthy, paunchy, balding, silver-haired men let their gaze wander over to North. They turned back to laugh at clever conversation at their tables, but drifted back to contemplate the slender young man at his physical peak. North saw several women at the bar staring hard at him and wondered if they all could be prostitutes in such an elegant establishment.

North found Gustavo Garcia seated at the bar.

"How we doing, buddy?" North said, as Garcia, exquisitely tailored in a gray Armani suit, embraced him.

"Good to see you, my friend," Garcia said. He looked around as if to offer the surroundings. "What do you think, Texas?"

"Very nice indeed," said North, taking in the paneled room and making eye contact with half a dozen women. Tasteful murals depicted Central Park in winter. "I don't believe we have anything quite like this back in Houston."

"That's the point, amigo. We have to expand your horizons."

North smiled. "How are our friends in Bogota?"

"Good. Life is good. I trust you got the wire transfer?"

"Indeed I did. God bless the Cayman Islands."

The bartender put two drinks before Garcia. He handed one to North.

"It's 30-year-old single malt. To our friendship."

"Salud!" said North.

Garcia put his glass high in the air. "To Antonio Gallegos!"

North laughed sharply. "Don't make me spit my 30-year-old Scotch." He took a sip. "But yes, may El Presidente live long and prosper."

North traded glances with a brunette at the far end of the bar. Her eyes looked blue from a distance, and her lips were full and sensual. He would have collected her if he weren't certain Garcia had special companionship planned for later in the evening. That's how it usually worked when North was posted in Bogata and Garcia was his fixer extraordinaire.

"Let me ask you, Gustavo. I don't want you to give away any trade secrets, but how did you manage to reach across the border?"

Garcia smiled. "Borders are for governments. When you have a business proposition, you find another businessman. The Venezuelan Air Force is always receptive to a respectful proposal. We saved them the loss of $1 billion worth of jet fighters, and they were more than happy to show their gratitude."

North laughed. "You should have seen the soldiers I brought with." His laughter built and he had to catch his breath. "They wanted to be right at the wire and I had to order them back to guard the rear." Garcia began to chuckle, too. "I felt like yelling, 'You're gonna get shot, you gung ho morons!'" He doubled over. People on either side of them turned around to look at the two well-dressed men in convulsive laughter.

"Treachery is an art where I come from," said Garcia.

"I learned from some of the best," North added.

******

Bobby Donuts looked at his cards again.

"What the fuck is wrong with this fucking guy," Bacciagaloop complained. "The bet is fifteen hundred. You in, or you out?"

Bobby Donuts grimaced. "Ah."

"This fuckin' guy," said Sally Beans. He was seated to Bacciagaloop's right and he was holding a very good hand.

Sammy Napolitano was lost in the Mets game. They held a 2-1 lead in the bottom of the eighth and no relievers worth a shit left in the bullpen. Classic Mets. As the host of the game in his bar, he had the luxury of not participating. Bacciagaloop was a grumpy poker player, and the fact that he rarely won made him intolerable.

Charlie Tuna forced the issue. "He's out."

"I'm in," said Bobby Donuts.

"Oh, *now* he's in," said Charlie Tuna.

"This fuckin' guy," said Sally Beans.

"Finally," said Bacciagaloop.

"In," said Charlie Tuna. He pushed cash to the center of the table.

"Call ya's," said Sally Beans.

"Queens," said Bacciagaloop.

"Eights over deuces," said Charlie Tuna.

"Ba fungool," said Bacciagaloop.

"Hey, don't worry about it," said Sally Beans, who proudly spread three tens on the table.

The three mobsters looked at Bobby Donuts, who looked back at them gripping his cards in his hand.

"You gonna look at us or you gonna throw 'em down?" said Bacciagaloop.

"So show us the freakin' cards," said Charlie Tuna.

"I got trip Jacks." He put them on the table.

"Trip Jacks," repeated Bacciagaloop.

"Three Jacks you had," said Charlie Tuna.

Bobby Donuts looked back and nodded at each of them.

From behind the bar, Sammy heard a rumble that could have been the subway, but he knew it was emanating from Sally Beans. *Oh shit*, he thought. *Here it comes.*

"Motherfucker!" Sally Beans bellowed. He hopped to his feet, his massive gut jiggling. He took a step toward Bobby Donuts, but Charlie Tuna got in the way. "You had trip Jacks and you had to fuckin' *think* about it!" He took another tiny step.

"Siddown, Beans," Bacciagaloop growled.

Looking over Charlie Tuna's head, Sally yelled: "I oughta put another fuckin' donut hole in your other fuckin' foot. Ya fuckin' mutt!"

Jesus, Mary and Joseph, Sammy thought. This life was supposed to be *glamorous*?

******

"This is fantastic, Gus," North said, sliding another piece of yellowtail sashimi with jalapeno into his mouth.

"Pace yourself, there's more coming out."

North locked eyes momentarily with a stylish redhead two tables away. She turned back to a discussion about distribution rights for the latest movie starring Vanessa Lamond. It was to begin shooting in a week in Spain.

"I wish they'd open a Nobu in Bogata," said Garcia.

"Then I'd never see you anymore, Gus."

Garcia looked past North. "Hey, here's Frank."

Frank Breslin was a lawyer who represented a smattering of upper echelon gangsters but mainly earned a sizeable living by introducing shady characters to shadowy operators. Stocky and silver-haired at 52, he was most interested in meeting Garcia's former running mate from Colombia, Matt North.

"Matt represents some powerful interests, Frank," Garcia said by way of introduction. Breslin nodded. He scanned the table.

"Did you get the black cod miso?" he asked.

"It's coming," Garcia said.

"Glad you guys started," said Breslin. "I got stuck at a deposition. Fuhgedaboudit."

"So I was explaining to Matt that you're a good guy to know," Garcia told Breslin.

"What I do, Matt, is put people like you together with other people like you with a corresponding need. Everybody's happy."

"That sounds like an important service," North said. "But what if I found people like me," he looked at Garcia, "on my own."

"You certainly could," Breslin said. "You could go that route. But here's what you get with me: I give you someone who has a track record in what it is you need. I know they can do the job. I know they have a reputation to uphold, which is very important. And I'll handle the negotiation. I just ask that everyone treats everyone else with professionalism and respect. Then it's a matter of getting everyone in the right location so they can do their thing."

"That's a nice business," North said. "I wish I knew you six months ago. But I'm glad to meet you now."

"Same here, Matt." Breslin looked back at the plates on the table. "Did we get the rock shrimp tempura? Oh, you got to have that."

******

The town car left Manhattan via the Triborough Bridge. North turned to watch the lights of the skyline.

The place certainly had magic, particularly when you drank the best liquor, ate the best food and, as they were about to do, indulged in prostitutes so talented you couldn't even buy them.

North was beginning to think he needed to have an apartment here, once everything came together. He had sampled splendors he hadn't even known existed, and he wanted more.

The car exited the parkway at La Guardia Airport and swung south. In a minute, they were in front of a nondescript row house.

"You're kidding," said North.

"Ah, you can't judge a book by its cover, Texas. There are some exquisitely talented young ladies in that building. Did you enjoy the meal tonight?"

"Absolutely."

"You will be no less satisfied here."

They were greeted inside by a most gracious woman in a business suit.

"We're so delighted you can be here this evening," she told North with a winsome smile. "I think you are in for a treat."

She led North upstairs and opened a door for him. The room was not large, but was richly furnished in the manner of an upscale Las Vegas hotel. Inside was a woman of perhaps 25, wearing a black cocktail dress. She looked as if she had just returned from the Oak Room.

She had a wholesome, girl-next-door look, if you happened to live in Cartagena. Brown-eyed and petite, she was more attractive by far than any of the women who had ogled North in Manhattan.

She smiled demurely and held out her hand. "Hi, my name is Sonia."

Chapter 19

A day after the six Colombians – members of the Navarro cartel from Cali – were executed in the stash house near La Guardia, a Chevy Suburban containing six men carrying Tec-9s pulled up in front of a social club on Roosevelt Avenue in Jackson Heights, Queens. Spraying automatic fire, they killed five men, members of the Marquez cartel from Santa Marta, in eastern Colombia, who were playing cards inside. A day later, the body of another Marquez soldier was found beside the Cross Island Parkway near the Throgs Neck Bridge. He had been tortured with a blowtorch, then shot.

The Intelligence Division had linked Yehuda Shapiro's cash-into-gold scheme with the Marquezes, so it didn't take Sherlock Holmes to see what was going on. Ross and Tori hustled back to New York. Their plane stopped in Greensboro, N.C., where it took on an Army general.

Ross called Sammy to get up to speed on the Colombian gang war ("This is Sammy. Don't leave a message. I don't return calls ..."). Eventually, Ross got through.

"Sammy, it's Ross."

"Ros-coe! You don't sound so good."

"I sound wonderful. I can't tell you how wonderful I sound."

"I'm happy for you, my man," Sammy said. "So let me guess: You want to talk about current events."

"Exactly."

"The handball courts at 9:30."

Ross and Sammy had spent a lot of time around the handball courts in East River Park as kids, but little of it involved playing handball. As rambunctious 12-year-olds, they stole equipment from other kids – gloves, bats, basketballs – and smoked illicit cigarettes at the handball courts.

After Arizona, Ross was chilled to the bone by a gloomy fall day in New York. By the time he got to Avenue D, he knew he had put on a couple layers too many. He crossed the busy street just ahead of a white cargo van and stopped to take off his denim jacket, the top layer. The van stopped, too, and Ross looked up just in time to see one of two men slip a hood over his head. They turned Ross horizontal, one man holding him by the armpits, the other by the legs. Ross was fascinated by how little one can resist with a hood over one's head. Suddenly he was cargo in a fast-moving vehicle.

Tori, tailing Ross, finally found her way across the street. No Ross. "Fuck!" She looked north, south, east. "Fucking fuck fuck fuck!"

******

They let Ross sit up, though with his hands bound behind his back, it wasn't a comfortable ride. He was still hooded, but he recalled that the van had no windows in the back anyway. They hadn't turned, so he imagined they were still headed uptown. No one spoke.

The van jogged slightly right and the ride got bumpier. Ross surmised they were getting on the FDR Drive – the entrance ramp was full of cavernous potholes – to go uptown or maybe to cut over to the Midtown

Tunnel. No, they check trucks for explosives at the tunnel – explain a hooded, trussed-up man in the back to the cops – so they'd take the 59th Street Bridge.

The van accelerated, telling Ross that they had gotten on the FDR. When it slowed and began creeping in traffic where 42nd Street should be, he was sure. They stayed on the FDR long enough to be up by the Triborough Bridge, leading to Queens or the Bronx. The FDR folds gently into the Harlem River Drive with just a twist, so Ross was convinced they had taken a cloverleaf onto the Triborough. Sure enough, the van paused just briefly, long enough for an E-Z Pass payment, and veered slightly right: Queens.

"You guys know any jokes?" Ross said. No answer.

"Come on, we can still be friends. No hard feelings." Silence.

******

Tori sat on a bench at 6th and Avenue D, staring vacantly at traffic. She willed herself not to think of Seattle. This was different, she told herself, Ross can handle himself. He'll be OK.

"Say, aren't you the Russian tennis player?" asked a man in a jogging suit unzipped to his solar plexus.

"Fuck off."

This couldn't be happening again. How could she have lost him? They must have taken him when passing traffic cut her off: a pro move. Her first impulse was to call Herron, but she persuaded herself to wait for a happy ending. If it were a hit, wouldn't they would have done him right then and there? Someone must have sent for him. Think, girl, think!

Sammy had arranged the meet. No one else could have known where Ross would be.

******

An aide led Dennis Bouton into Tom Catapano's West Wing office.

"You look worried, Dennis."

"*Concerned* is the word I would use. You've heard about the Rucker encounter?"

Catapano arranged his thick mop of brown hair, leaned back in his desk chair and put his feet up. "Oh yes. The Rucker ruckus. That's the last face time he'll ever see. I know they do things differently down there in Texas, but this guy's a real loon."

Bouton laughed, instantly relieved that Catapano could make light. "Tom, this guy is a real loose cannon. We can keep him away from the President, but he's got cowboys running around in New York – I dare not share the details – but it's not good and he's got to be contained. He needs to be persuaded to fold his tents and ride home."

Catapano smiled widely. "That's why we have the S.E.C."

Bouton grinned. "Ouch. Game, set and match."

"See how easy it is?" Catapano said. "He's a giant liability, and he knows it. Oh, he'll try a thing or two. We led him on about getting a piece of the Maracaibo oil, but really, how likely is that to happen. I mean, come on."

"Right."

"He'll appeal to me, but he's dead to us. His name's been erased. I never start a relationship like that without having two moves worked out in advance." Catapano beamed.

"Wow, Tom. Don't ever let me get on your bad side."

Catapano chuckled. "We hold all the cards. We're the house. They have to play what they're dealt."

******

"We're going to release your hands and remove

the hood. OK?" The English was Spanish-accented.

"Sure. I'm good with that," Ross said. He was very good with that, having spent 90 minutes bumping along in the van breathing through some sort of acrylic blend. He felt the plastic bands snap and then the cool breeze on his face as the hood was lifted. He didn't open his eyes all at once, but even still, the light took time to adjust to.

Ross was on the patio of a manor house on a large wooded property; he guessed some posh part of Long Island: Muttontown or Mill Neck. The fall leaves were brilliant. He could smell a wood fire burning somewhere inside. If it came to it, he would much prefer being executed here than at the dingy *World Famous* Agave Lounge, in a scorched place where things go to die.

He recognized the man who had surprised him with the hood, and he guessed the two other Latinos were part of the delivery crew. The fourth man, dapper in a shearling coat and matching brown cowboy hat, dismissed the others in Spanish.

"I apologize for this rough treatment, Mr. Walton. Or should I call you Detective Walton?"

"Ross is good enough. What shall I call you?" The man was so well-groomed that Ross felt an impulse to smooth his hair, mussed by the 90 minutes under wrap.

"I am Emilio Navarro. Perhaps you have heard of me."

"I've heard of your drug cartel. The Navarro Cartel of Cali and Queens, N.Y."

"So they say." A maid brought a tray with coffee and a pair of cigars. "Smoke?"

"Mind if I have one of my own?" Ross asked, fishing for his pack of cigarettes. Thank God for the crush-proof box.

******

Tori found Sammy Napolitano where Ross had

found him just a few days earlier. Sammy sat reading *The Daily Racing Form*. Johnny looked up from *The Post*. Tori took off her BFD hat and let her hair fall. The men stared. Tori said nothing.

"I know who you are," Sammy said finally.

"Where's Ross?"

"He said you were gorgeous but, *marrone*." Sammy leaned around to check with Johnny.

"*Una Madonna*," said Johnny.

"Where's Ross, Sammy?"

"Sit, dear, sit," Sammy offered. "Johnny, get the lady something. What would you like, sweetheart? Espresso? We can make you some tea. Something stronger?"

Between clenched teeth, Tori spat: "Where … the fuck … is Ross?"

"He's safe. C'mon. We've been friends since we were too young to jerk off – excuse the expression. I wouldn't let anything happen to him."

"If anything –" she started over. "Someone hurt someone very important to me once. I found this motherfucker, and I broke his arms. Then I broke his legs. Then I broke his ribs and sat on his chest until he smothered."

Sammy's expression froze, but then he smiled a big used-car-dealer smile. "Doll, he's in very safe hands. Probably the safest place in the city. I promise. Look at this face. Would I lie to you, sweetheart?"

Thick mustache, jet-black hair, piercing dark eyes, bent Roman nose. Sure, a face to bet the house on.

"Sammy, if he's not back safe and sound by sundown, I'm coming for you."

******

Emilio Navarro explained the predicament: The rival Marquez cartel suspected Navarro of eliminating the cash cow, Yehuda Shapiro. Now there was a gang war that was costing lives. More important, it was *muy malo* for business.

"Javier Marquez is a psychopath. It is nothing for him to slaughter a roomful of people. He'd think nothing of making his moves in the streets, where innocent women and children could be hit in crossfire. I brought you here, Ross, to tell you that I will use all the resources of my organization to help you find who killed this Shapiro. Otherwise, the full attention of the city is on these Colombian *animales*."

"I know it wasn't you. Someone hired mercenaries, ex-soldiers, to clip the guy. There's more to come, and it will be bad news for the city if I don't find who's behind this. I would very much like your help, Emilio."

"See," Navarro said. "We're not such bad guys."

Ross wasn't quite sure what the proper response was, so he just smiled.

"Tell me, Emilio," said Ross. "You're a man of the world. Who would hire former soldiers – Special Forces soldiers – to kill a jeweler mixed up with the Marquez cartel?"

Navarro puffed his cigar. Everything about him seemed unhurried and measured. "You don't know?"

"Well, no," said Ross, wondering what should be so obvious.

"Your government would do that."

The wind kicked up and as the trees shook, Ross noticed a man in camouflage hidden in the woods. Navarro gestured with his cigar. "One of my men. It is very dangerous for me to be here. My men will return you to the city now, but unfortunately, for security, you must wear the hood."

Chapter 20

Lyle Rucker stepped from his Gulfstream jet. He had promised Debbie a Caribbean getaway, but he'd neglected to mention that this particular island, about 200 miles north of Caracas, was largely given over to a Venezuelan Air Force base. La Orchila also boasted a lavish seaside complex that Rucker wasn't about to tell his wife belonged to the president of Venezuela, Antonio Gallegos de la Paz. What Rucker loved about Debbie, nearly as much as her flawless, youthful body, was her ability to accept the luxury in which Rucker immersed her without asking any bothersome questions.

A white sedan approached from where its occupants had watched Rucker's jet touch down. Matt North, walked over and shook hands with the men who got out. He led a tall man dressed casually to Rucker.

"Mr. Rucker, this is Colonel Manuel Torregrossa."

"Colonel, it's my pleasure, sir."

"The pleasure is all mine, Mr. Rucker. President Gallegos is very honored to host you here. He extends his greetings to you and Mrs. Rucker."

"Please tell the President that I am deeply grateful, and that I look forward to a long and fruitful relationship," Rucker said.

"And now, my people will move your party into

the presidential compound. I hope you will find the accommodations comfortable."

The accommodations were more than comfortable. Through French doors in the bedroom lay a panoramic view of the pink-sand beach. "Oh Ly, it's beautiful," Debbie observed.

"Darlin', I'm afraid I'm going to have a fairly long meeting here. But we've got a couple of hours to kill beforehand. Did you bring it?"

"You know I did, sugar. Did you take your pill?"

"Took it on the plane. Cocked and loaded."

"Well then, pardon me." Debbie disappeared into the bathroom. Rucker undressed and slipped between the sheets. A minute later Debbie reappeared wearing the familiar blue-and-white-and-stars outfit. She high-kicked and cheered: "Go Dallas Cowboys! Go Cowboy team!"

******

The Colombians dropped Ross in Times Square with the number for a contact, should he need to reach out for the Navarros, named Luis. He checked his cell: 26 missed calls, all from Tori. He dialed her.

"Jesus Christ, are you OK?" she said.

"I was taken on a little sightseeing tour," said Ross. "Actually, they didn't allow any *seeing*, but it was quite pleasant. I'm fine."

"Where are you?"

"I'm by TKTS in the middle of Times Square."

"Don't move, I'm on my way."

Ross smoked a cigarette and watched the tourists mill around the ticket center. He wanted to get a good look at regular, law-abiding people. The closest he'd come to them in a couple of years were the tattooed, pierced, stapled denizens of Flynn's in the wee hours. These people looked fresh off the farm – fattened for slaughter and dressed for a pancake breakfast. He was fascinated, and he suddenly wondered if any of them were from Roscoe.

Tori was there within 10 minutes, causing male heads to swivel violently as she moved through the crowd. She wordlessly clamped Ross in a tight embrace.

Though Tori didn't much like coffee, she loved the paper coffee cups with faux Greek lettering that were as much a part of New York as street crime. Ross told her that the message on the cups – "We Are Happy to Serve You" – was the NYPD motto.

"Yeah, like hell it is," she said. "More like: We Look Forward to Collecting Our Pension After 20."

"And buy a bar in Coral Gables," Ross added. Tori grabbed his face with both hands and kissed him. It was a new, and not unpleasurable experience to be kissed by his partner, and he involuntarily imagined being kissed by one of his former sour-breath backups.

"I can't believe I had just told you that fucking kidnapping story and ..." she didn't finish.

"No stories with unhappy endings from now on, OK?" he said.

"I was so worried. Don't ever do that again." She held up a fist. He wished they were back in the desert, playing catch-me-and-you-can-have-me. "If you hadn't showed by sundown I was going to fucking kill Sammy."

"You didn't — "

"I sure did. He's down there in his bar trying to decide what suit he should wear at his wake. He set you up, Ross."

Ross described his abduction and told her about Emilio Navarro, his terrific grooming and his offer of assistance. It was well worth being snatched off the streets.

"Sammy may seem sleazy to you, but we go way back. He helps out when he can. He's always got his ear to the street. Always. He's like the ambassador for the downtown wiseguys."

"He's a lucky man," said Tori. "If the Colombians had made a day out of it, Sammy was history."

They were drinking weak coffee from a pushcart on the west side of Broadway when Herron called them in.

******

Ross, Tori and Herron huddled around a computer screen studying a very short sequence of footage from a subway surveillance camera.

"This is about the best we can tune it up," said the technician at the keyboard. The footage, shot from a camera looking down the passageway between Fifth and Sixth Avenues – where Yehuda Shapiro was gunned down – showed three men wearing felt dress hats, scarves and flipped-up collars.

"They're way overdressed," Ross said. "It was a pretty mild night." They appear at the midway point in the tunnel, where it turns about 15 degrees, and walk by.

"Not much to go on," Tori said. The tech had it looped; the threesome walk close and then reappear at the beginning of their stroll.

"Hardly any faces, between the hats and the scarves," Ross said.

They kept watching: Closer, closer, closer, back to the beginning. Closer, closer, closer, back to Go.

"I can make them go backwards, if that'll help?" the technician said. The other three ignored him.

"Was this monitored?" Tori asked.

"No," Herron said. "They've got hundreds of these cameras all over the subway system. Maybe a couple thousand. There's no way we have enough eyes to watch them – particularly late at night."

"Hey," Ross said.

"What is it?" Tori asked.

"That last bit, when they're close – the light is better."

"Yeah?" the tech said.

"Stop it at that point, when they're in the good

light, and then give me the best look at their shoes that you got." Herron and Tori looked at each other, then at Ross.

"Their shoes?" the tech asked.

"Trust me," Ross replied.

The tech cued it up, then panned down and dialed up until the pixels failed to hold a discernible picture.

"That's about the best I can get it." He squinted. "Some kind of hiking boots?" The three bent in for a closer look. Clearly two of them were wearing exotic boots.

"What do we know about Bozzo's boots?" Ross asked.

"Bought them at a discount place in Canarsie," Herron said. "Nothing special."

"Can you print a picture of the boots?" Ross asked.

******

Herron sent them upstairs to see someone named Lowery in forensics. Lowery turned out to be a woman of about 50, tall and sturdy in a white lab coat.

"Whaddaya got? Latents? Plastic?"

"Huh?"

"Your prints? Did they dust it, or did the shoe make a depression, like in mud? Whaddaya got?" Tori handed her the picture from the subway camera.

"What the hell is this?" Lowery asked. She made a face like she'd been handed curdled milk.

"No prints. Shoes," said Ross. "Those are our perps in a murder. They're wearing some kind of fancy boots. We need a shoe ID." Lowery made an impatient face. Ross looked at Tori, whose eyes were narrowing.

"What's your name?" Tori asked.

"Lowery."

"Your first name." Lowery looked to Ross and made the impatient face again.

- 140 -

"Mildred," she spat.

"OK, Mildred. I'm Tori and this is Ross. We're on a very important case that is so secret we report to the commissioner. Jack Steele? You know that name?" Mildred was stone faced. "Now follow along, Mildred. If you continue to give us your what-a-big-bitch-I-am attitude your next move may be *selling* shoes." They waited while Mildred made the calculations. Finally, she grinned and took the picture from Ross.

"Yeah, these are pretty exotic." She studied the picture closer.

"These guys in the pictures are former Special Forces. So we think it's some kind of survival boot," said Ross. She took another glance.

"Look, I can't really help you with this. We study prints. Shoe prints, not shoes. They get left at crime scenes. The shoes themselves – they usually *leave* the crime scene with the perp. If your perp had made a footprint in blood, you'd be driving to his house by now. Our database is built for prints, not loafers."

"So there's nothing you can do?" asked Ross.

"Me? No. But what I suggest you do is go to Eddie's Army-Navy on 14th. Between Seventh and Eighth. They know from hiking boots. Ask for Lem and tell him Mildred from Police Plaza sent you."

Twenty minutes later, they were telling Lem that Mildred had sent them.

"Mildred?" he said. "Nice lady."

Tori and Ross looked at each other. "Um, yeah, OK," said Tori. "We might not be talking about the same Mildred."

Minutes later, Lem was flipping through catalogues. "Italian, I think." He stopped flipping. He looked back to the photo. "Yes, that's it. Zoltani mountain boots." Tori and Ross took a look for themselves. Bingo.

"They have a great toe. Lightweight, waterproof, very balanced. Do you know who loves these?" he asked.

"No, who?" said Tori.

"Special Forces guys in Afghanistan. Along the border with Pakistan where it's really rocky."

Chapter 21

"He wants to see us," Tori said.

"OK, he wants to see us," Ross replied with a shrug. "Where is he?"

"Philadelphia."

"You're shitting me."

"He wants us to come to Philadelphia," Tori said. "He doesn't want to talk on the phone."

Ross looked around the small office that contained the Intelligence Division. A clock on the wall said 12:30; a clock on another wall said 12:50.

"Jesus H. – is this gonna be another dead end?"

"This guy's solid. I've worked with him. He was at Tora Bora. He has a pair of the freakin' boots, all right?" She stood up straight so that Ross had to tilt his head slightly to look up into her eyes. He knew the look. Ross had come to think of it as *the dead look*. They were going to Philadelphia.

"Can I grab a cup of coffee first? I've had kind of a busy day, being kidnapped and all."

"Did they beat you?"

"No."

"Abuse you in any way?"

"No, they were quite pleasant, actually."

"So you had a nice outing in the country." She shook her head in disgust. "Grow a pair."

"Wow," he protested. "An hour ago you were concerned I was dead."

She put her nose up to his, drill-sergeant style. "Yeah, well you're not. And one more thing. We have to get there before the museum closes."

They hustled out to the Impala. Ross protested enough that Tori allowed him to get a hot dog from one of the carts on Chambers Street. They crept west across the fat chunk of impossibly congested streets that make up Lower Manhattan. Trucks lurched into intersections with no hope of advancing and sat there blocking the box as the light changed. Ross sat on Broome Street and watched a light go green, then yellow and red, without moving an inch. He wondered if spy rules applied to truckers who didn't give a shit about fellow motorists.

"Fuck this," he said. He flicked the lights and siren. Magically, cars going north squeezed ahead another foot, giving the truck six feet of extra clearance. Ross drove wide left onto the crosswalk, hung two wheels on the curb and cleared the intersection. He glanced in his rear view and saw that a cab had come with him.

"One day the last car will pull into place and they'll need big helicopters to fix this mess," Tori observed.

"I already made my one trip to New Jersey for the year. I really don't need this shit."

"Are you getting old? That doesn't sound like someone who slept in crack houses to catch a killer. Do you want names? Do you want to keep your city safe?"

"Yeah."

"Then do your crazy New York driver stuff and get us out of here. Or I could put in a word and see if Bill Herron can get your old job back for you."

"Oh, that's just cruel."

They pushed their way west on Spring Street until wide lanes of traffic congealed like frozen grease. "The Holland is fucked," Ross concluded. He hit the lights, camera, action again and peeled off, headed toward West

Street.

"Good," Tori said. "Get us out of this shithole."

"Next stop, Aspen," Ross said. "Did I tell you I can't ski?"

Traffic crept, but in comparison to the death march through the tunnel to Jersey, they were making warp speed. They drove south, past the big hole in the ground that had once provided office space for 40,000 people. Ross thought that one day he should count up the number of friends who had died there that bright day in September.

The Impala slipped down into the entrance to the Brooklyn-Battery Tunnel as if it disappeared through a hole in time.

"Nice," said Tori.

"The secret trap door," said Ross. He could relax a little, having outflanked the daily blockage that, if Manhattan were a person, would surely lead to cardiac arrest.

Ross didn't feel comfortable with *get there before the museum closes*. Once on the Brooklyn-Queens Expressway, a hellish elevated stretch of moon-sized potholes and abrupt twists, Ross decided to make up time. He drove absurdly close to the backs of cars in his lane and floated over a lane, bobbing and weaving across three lanes of traffic, building enough speed that drivers paying attention to their rear views simply got out of the way of the lunatic about to ram them from behind. Ross noticed someone was using him for a blocker, much as the taxi had slipped behind him as he bulled his way across Broome Street.

They crossed the Verrazano Narrows Bridge out of Brooklyn. He slugged his way across the Staten Island Expressway and down the West Shore Expressway, past the world's largest heap of garbage, the Fresh Kills landfill.

 Something wasn't right.

They crossed over to New Jersey on the narrow

Outerbridge Crossing, named not for its geographic significance but for some guy named Outerbridge. Once on Route 440, Ross swung over to the far right lane and dropped to 50 mph.

"What are you doing?" asked Tori.

"Silver Lexus," he said. "I noticed him on the BQE. He can't hit the brakes now, he'll be blown." They both watched as the car glided by at no more than 60. The windows were tinted. It looked like every other Japanese car on the highway.

Ross took the exit for the New Jersey Turnpike and decelerated up the ramp. He pulled over well short of the toll booth.

"We'll give him a few minutes. If he's not a tail, then he'll be gone. If we see him again, he's for real. New York plate. Did you get any numbers?"

"Last three are 339. That's about it. No Semper Fi stickers; no Jesus fish."

Ross pulled onto the road ahead of a double-semi.

"Fuck it, let's go. We've got shotguns in the trunk."

Traffic was thick but moving with only occasional taps on the brakes. Ross kept to a steady 75, more or less sticking to the generally accepted rules because of the abundance of state troopers. He and Tori scanned ahead for the silver Lexus. Ross kept an extra special eye on the rear and side mirrors, just in case.

They cruised through the industrial forest of smokestacks and mountain-sized tanks that is the face of North Jersey. Tori would have napped through it if they weren't dealing with an orange threat level.

"Have you ever been to Philadelphia?" Tori asked.

"Yeah, a couple of times. It's OK."

"Well that's a ringing endorsement."

"What can I say? It's old and historical. But so is New York. The people are cranky and they talk funny. They do this weird thing with O's. And their sports fans are obnoxious."

"You just described about every city in the country."

"Hey!" Ross pointed ahead. Tori spotted a silver Lexus, poking along in the right lane. As they drew closer, she could make out the last numbers of the license plate: 339.

Ross fell in behind the Lexus.

"Now what?" asked Tori. The car windows were opaque; there was no telling who was in there.

"I'm just gonna break their balls a little." He had the Impala about three feet from the rear bumper of the Lexus. "We don't really have time to screw around with — " The Lexus accelerated and sped across three lanes to the far left and out of sight.

******

They drove over the Benjamin Franklin Bridge from Camden, over the Delaware River to Philadelphia. The bridge deposited them on Vine Street, a crosstown expressway, with shabby warehouses and weathered Federal style buildings on the right and the highrise skyline on the left.

At Broad Street, Ross looked south to City Hall, which wore a giant statue of William Penn like a big bronze hat. Until the 80s, no building could go higher than William Penn's head. But that rule had clearly fallen by the wayside.

Ross took a slight right onto Benjamin Franklin Parkway, which would take them to their destination, the Philadelphia Museum of Art – just beyond the Benjamin Franklin Institute.

"Why didn't they just name the city Benjamin Franklin and save themselves the trouble of naming everything in it after him?" Ross said.

The Art Museum was a huge rambling building with a Greek Parthenon façade that looked down the broad, tree-lined parkway toward the city's center. They took in the vista, looking down the steep steps made famous by Rocky, the most famous fictional Philadelphian.

"I love Rocky," said Tori. "He reminds me of you, except he's got an intellect."

"Thanks. Didn't Rocky eat paste?" Ross affected a deep, Rocky-like voice. "Yo, I'm poor and stupid but if I keep hitting this side of meat here" – he threw a couple of combinations – "I'll be the champ. Yo, Cuff. Yo, Link."

They were meeting Tori's contact in front of a painting called *Prometheus Bound.* Jerry Sheehan was a former Green Beret who had become an investment banker.

They found the painting on the second floor.

"Is this some kind of message, meeting here?" asked Ross, as he studied the enormous canvas. "This thing is fucking spooky!"

"Peter Paul Rubens," Tori read off the plaque. "Made in Southern Netherlands (modern Belgium). Begun circa 1611-12, completed by 1618."

The painting depicted a mammoth eagle plucking the liver out of the side of Prometheus, the character in Greek mythology who stole fire from the gods and gave it to man. Prometheus was chained to a boulder. The eagle had a giant talon planted on Prometheus' face for leverage as it tugged at the liver. His punishment was to endure this giant-eagle liver feast every day after his liver regenerated.

"There's a bedtime tale for the children," said Ross. "Go to bed or a giant eagle will rip out your liver. Night-night."

Tori nodded. "It's a little grim."

"And Ray Charles was a little blind."

Tori looked past Ross at a man in a well-tailored suit. Tori hugged him and introduced him to Ross.

"What do you think of Prometheus here?" Sheehan asked them.

"Cheerful," said Ross. "It definitely brightened up

my day."

Sheehan ignored him and spoke to Tori. "I loved coming here as a kid. This painting fascinated me. They say Rubens was making a statement about the suffering of the artist."

As the three of them studied the 400-year-old painting, a boy of 4 or 5 wandered over and gazed wide-eyed.

"Frankie, get away from there," his mother called.

They talked as they wandered through the galleries.

"What are you doing these days, Jerry?" Tori asked.

"I sell energy derivatives on the futures market," he said. "It's complicated, but I do OK." He laughed. "Actually, I make gobs of money." His short hair was immaculately barbered. His suit looked expensive; his black wingtips gleamed.

"Jerry, I need some names," said Tori. "We're looking for two of your guys who've gone over the wall. We've got two bodies and we expect more."

Sheehan folded his arms and looked down at wingtips. "I've got two guys in mind. They were good soldiers, but they bugged out after Tora Bora. We all bugged a little after that."

"What do you mean 'bugged'?" Ross asked.

"They were good soldiers. They just lost it. One of them claimed he'd shot bin Laden and killed him. Saw his head explode through his sniper scope. But we never found a body. There wasn't much to go on. His sergeant backed him up, and it became really sensitive. DOD at really high levels didn't want anyone saying Osama had gone down. I mean, we hung a lot of war on the need to get him, so if he was already dead … "

"I see," said Tori. "But how did they bug?"

"They really put the clamps to these guys to shut up. And if you get a soldier's back up, well, then you've got trouble. They were versus the Army and it just built.

Then it was a vendetta. They wrote them up for all sorts of petty bullshit until they concocted some questionable charges that they'd fired into a village full of civilians. I didn't believe it, but it was enough to run them out of the service with bad paper."

"Bad paper?" Ross asked.

"You don't want anything short of an honorable discharge. If you're a veteran, and you come out with anything less, it draws questions. It's tough to get a job. In the case of these guys, they were forced to leave with an undesirable discharge. That's not as bad as a dishonorable or bad conduct discharge – they need to court-martial you for that. But you're kind of screwed coming out with bad paper. Particularly if you're Special Forces. People tend to assume you're a psycho."

"But these guys didn't do anything wrong?" Tori asked.

"Not really," Sheehan said. "They pissed off the wrong people." He walked over to study a van Gogh, *Rain*. The description noted that van Gogh had painted this view from the window of the hospital in southern France where he had gone after a mental breakdown. Angry slashes of white represented rain falling across a turquoise field of wheat. The sadly beautiful painting by poor tortured Vincent made Ross think of Prometheus and his sad, tortured liver. Now he remembered what he'd forgotten to tell Tori: Philadelphia was a downer.

"The thing is," Sheehan said, his eyes still locked on the van Gogh, "these guys are in for anything now and they don't cast the Special Forces – me – in an especially good light. Green Beret, Rangers, Delta Force, the SEALs, are all selective as hell. You have to be tough and you have to have a good head as well. Remember Jesse Ventura, the wrestler who was elected governor of Minnesota? He was a SEAL. We don't need the public to think we're all psychos when we come home."

"Jerry," Tori said softly, "I need names."

"Skip McKenzie," he said. "Jason Hummel." He

looked back at *Rain.* "Those are your boys."

Chapter 22

Herron's analysts quickly determined that the two former Green Berets – Michael "Skip" McKenzie and Jason "Ironhead" Hummel – had been making ATM withdrawals from a Bank of America kiosk next to the Hotel Pennsylvania on Eighth Avenue. The withdrawals began a day before Shapiro was shot and were still continuing, the latest coming a day ago.

Tori and Ross had barely gotten off the Benjamin Franklin Parkway and back on the Benjamin Franklin Bridge when Heron called with the news.

"Hot fucking damn!" Tori said as she hung up. "Way to go, Jerry!"

"Way to go Tori and Ross," Ross said.

"Way to go, us."

He looked at her. "I like the sound of that. *Us.*"

They decided to look for a diner to celebrate – once they got beyond the grim confines of Camden. Ross could imagine a modernized Greek myth in which Prometheus is forced to walk from one end of Admiral Wilson Boulevard to another, for all eternity.

"There's one," Tori said, pointing up ahead. It was the Benjamin Franklin Diner. "Now it's starting to get a little creepy," she said.

Tori ordered a Greek salad, which turned out to be large enough to have a couple of Greeks hidden in it. The waitress gave Ross a look when he ordered a "Philly cheese steak."

"I think they just call them cheese steaks around here, genius," Tori said.

"Whatever."

Tori smiled at him. "I got to hand it to you, the shoes were a brilliant move. You cracked it open, partner."

Ross' eyes widened. "Thanks. That's the nicest thing you've ever said to me."

"See? It's not all tough love."

"I'll take whatever love I can get."

"We'll see about that."

Ross picked over Tori's salad – she'd left all the olives and feta cheese. He said that it seemed odd that a Greek salad didn't have a giant liver in it. He had several cups of bitter, burnt diner coffee for the ride home. As they walked across the parking lot, a silver car pulled in. A Lexus. Ross reached for the Beretta. The Lexus passed by. It had Jersey plates.

"I think you were being paranoid," Tori said. "You're not the only lunatic driver around here. So somebody wanted to keep up with you."

"If they're really after you, you're not paranoid," Ross said. "That car was tailing us. It was no coincidence."

They made it up the Turnpike and through the Holland Tunnel without a tail or apocalyptic traffic, although the refineries in Linden were especially pungent.

"That smells like boiled death," said Tori.

"That's Eau du New Jersey," Ross explained.

They drove easily across town and headed to Police Plaza to look through the data the analysts had mined.

At 11 o'clock, Herron summoned his clandestine cops into his office. The news was on.

"Now we have news of a startling arrest in the killing last week of a Diamond District jeweler in the subway. Andrew Kramer has the story from Clifton, New Jersey. Andrew ..."

"Sylvia, just minutes ago, highly armed cops from the NYPD, the Passaic County Sheriff's Office and the Clifton Police Department raided this house on the city's west side and arrested a former Navy SEAL." The report now showed footage of Kozloski being herded out of the yellow house by a phalanx of cops wearing futuristic protective gear. "The man, identified as William Kozloski, 35, offered no resistance, although a pit bull in the house had to be put down."

"Well that was inevitable," Ross said.

"Kozloski was being held for questioning about the gangland-style murder of Yehuda Shapiro, owner of this 47th Street shop, in a Manhattan subway passage one late night last week. Manhattan Homicide Chief Arthur Borrelli said charges are pending."

Herron muted the TV. "And that should put a stop to the Colombian war," he said. "I'll have another team find McKenzie and Hummel and stick with them. The Hotel Penn would probably fit their budget."

"Right by the train station," Ross said. "Anything goes sour and they're out of town. It's where I'd stay."

"Unless they're in a safe house," said Tori.

"We won't know until we ask the questions," said Herron.

"Old-fashioned shoe leather," said Ross.

"Maybe Lowery could help us with the shoe leather," Tori said, rolling her eyes.

Herron grinned. "Piece of work, huh?"

"She's not for everybody," Ross said.

"Is she for anybody?" Tori asked.

******

Rucker and North sipped Cognac on the patio of President Gallegos' villa on La Orchila. The Caribbean was unseen in the dark, but its gentle wash provided a soothing soundtrack to their conversation.

"We'll touch down in Teterboro on the way back," Rucker said.

"Good. My team is still in place. We can have this done in a couple of days."

"Nice rebound, Matt. Thanks to you and your connections we're about to make more money than either of us ever dreamed of. We'll each be able to retire to our own islands like this one."

"That's what makes our country great, sir. The opportunity."

"You got that right." The sound of the water was soothing. Rucker hadn't been able to resist a quick dip in the turquoise surf after his pharmaceutically enhanced ravishing of Debbie. She was thrilled that he had joined her. She loved the water and swam every day in the indoor lap pool he had built for her. He couldn't imagine a woman could look sexier in a one-piece bathing suit.

"The beauty of this is we don't have to deal with those chicken shits in the White House," said Rucker. "I'm gonna have Dennis Bouton's head on a plate some day soon."

"What a candy ass," said North.

"The great lesson I've learned in the business world," Rucker told North, "is that the ones who truly make it – not just hang on, but kick everyone else's butt – are the ones willing to do what no one else would. I sleep like a bear in the dead of winter. If you want to get ahead, you have to put it on the line. No risk, no reward. You make a decision and you face forward."

"Big risk, big reward," North added.

"Exactly right," Rucker said. "Exactly dadgum right."

Debbie emerged from the villa.

"And speaking of the big reward," said Rucker.

"Why thank you, sugar." She threw her arms around him. "I don't know what you boys were talking about, but thank you anyway."

"We were talking about how the ones who achieve greatness are willing to do what no one else is," said North.

"Absolutely," she said. "My Daddy was a good man. Worked for the railroad. The Santa Fe. Steady as they come. But risks?" She wrinkled her nose. "No, sir. He's got his pension and his little house in Denton.

"Now take Lyle here. One of the biggest oilmen in Houston. And started with nothing but his two hands."

"That's about it, darlin'."

"When the going gets rough, Lyle gets rougher," she said.

Rucker chuckled. "Yes, ma'am. I guess you can say that."

"What about you, Mr. North. When the going gets rough, do you get rougher?"

North nodded. "You might say that."

******

Ross and Tori got back to the apartment just before midnight. Ross headed to the roof for a smoke.

"I'll come with," Tori said. They emerged from the stairwell looking east toward a dazzling chunk of Manhattan's midsection.

"Wow," said Tori.

"Yes," Ross said. "Wow." He turned her toward him and kissed her. "Wow," he repeated.

She gave him a sly smile, backed away and launched into series of air kicks and punches. He watched her dance in and out of the shadows on the rooftop.

"You really ought to be doing this," Tori called out. "If you don't practice, it doesn't do much good."

"Tomorrow," Ross said. "I'm starting tomorrow."

He watched the lights of the city and looked at the three or four stars strong enough to compete.

"Wow," he said.

Chapter 23

The waitress placed the plate brimming with boiled, poached and fried breakfast items before Ironhead Hummel. Skip McKenzie had a bowl of Irish oatmeal and considered his partner's mountain of food.

"That's probably enough calories to last you through next week," McKenzie said.

Hummel mumbled a protest through a mouthful of black pudding. He swallowed. "I couldn't eat any of that stuff in Colombia."

"Venezuela."

"Whatever. You know the rule, when you've got good food, eat it."

The waitress approached. "How's everything luv? Are you liking the Irish breakfast?" They had established while ordering that she was from County Galway. Everyone who worked in the hotel was from County Something or Other. Hummel grunted and shook his head vaguely to indicate his intense pleasure.

"More coffee, gentlemen?"

"Sure," McKenzie said. He watched her walk off.

"The man gave us another job," McKenzie said. Hummel paused for air.

"Yeah?"

"Yeah. I had to meet him at an airfield in Jersey."

"I love that guy."

"Yeah, this is a pretty sweet deal."

"How soon?"

"The quicker the better."

"Do we have to leave afterward?" Hummel asked, rapidly clearing his plate of eggs and sausages. "I fucking love New York."

"Yeah, we need to go. We're pushing it here."

A few steps away, Detective Roy Fitzsimmons sat at the adjacent hotel bar sipping coffee. He texted his partner, Tony Gargiulio, lingering at the hotel entrance: "Wrapping up bfast. Get ready."

A dozen blocks away, Ross and Tori inspected the door to Room 1620 of the Hotel Concordia. It had taken Fitzsimmons and Gargiulio a day to determine that the hitmen were careful enough to avoid banking where they slept.

"There." Tori pointed to a slender copper filament. They opened the door with the keycard the manager had made for them.

"Got it," said Ross, depositing the tiny wire in a baggie as he noted its position tucked into the doorjam a third of the way up from the floor.

The room looked barely lived in. The two ex-soldiers clearly had told housekeeping to stay away, and had made the beds as crisply as if they were expecting inspection. It seemed as if they had anticipated someone rifling through their room. The trash held just the usual bathroom detritus and discarded convenience-store packaging.

Ross texted a single word "in" to Fitzsimmons and received a quick reply: "20 minutes."

Though the hitmen had spent 10 nights in the room, nothing was unpacked; their bags – normal tourist luggage – were zipped and ready to go.

"Christ, we could never get this back right," Tori said, studying the bags.

"Hold on," said Ross. The bags had zippered pockets. One was crammed with tourist pamphlets and business cards for Midtown restaurants. From the second bag, he extracted a folder. "Presto!" Tori looked over his shoulder as he leafed through: a picture of a dapper Latino man, pictures of a house, streets, utility boxes, maps of a neighborhood in Douglaston, an expensive section of Queens favored by well-paid city employees who wanted the comfort of the suburbs but required a city address.

Taking care to keep the documents in the same order, Ross photographed each page and returned the file to the pocket of the bag. Ross' phone vibrated. The text read: "On the move."

******

"I don't get it," Ross told Herron. "How does Shapiro lead to this Colon guy?"

"You can't connect the dots until you have them all," Herron said.

"Shapiro worked with the Marquez cartel," said Tori.

"Right," Ross said.

"And this dirty cop – what's his name?" said Tori.

"Margolis," said Herron.

"Margolis grew up with Shapiro and carried water for all the Colombians," she said.

"Yeah," said Herron, "papal nuncio to the cocaine industry. The mercs probably did him, too. But now we jump the border to Venezuela. Eduardo Colon was a justice minister in the last administration. He fled Gallegos, and since he's been in New York, he's been El Presidente's biggest critic. The White House loves to trot him out when they want to denounce Gallegos, which is about every hour."

"Is Gallegos that bad?" Ross asked.

"Yes and no. No worse than any of the other blowhards down there, I guess. Only he's got a lot of oil, a lot of money to throw around and a lot of juice in South

America and the Caribbean, and that makes him a bit of a threat. He's cozy with Cuba and the Russians just to piss off Washington. And we've spent a lot of money down there trying to push the Venezuelans toward getting rid of him themselves."

"So the Venezuelans hired the two cement heads to hit some Colombian wannabes and now a dissident?" said Tori. "That doesn't make much sense."

"No, it doesn't," Herron said. "And that's why we need more dots."

******

Fitzsimmons and Gargiulo were perplexed. They had tailed McKenzie and Hummel to a parking garage on Second Avenue, where they had picked up a limo and driven it to The Pierre, on East 61st Street opposite Central Park. As they pulled in front of the elegant landmark hotel, five Middle Eastern men in casual but expensive-looking clothes filed outside and got into the limo. Hummel – distinguishable even from a distance at night because of his 6-foot-5, 240-pound stature – opened the door for them and took a briefcase from one of the passengers as they all climbed aboard.

The two Intel Division detectives followed the limo across town to the Hustler Club across from the West Side piers in the West 50s. They valet parked the limo and the whole band, including McKenzie and Hummel, entered the club – Hummel still carrying the briefcase. Gargiulo documented the outing with a high-speed camera. They debated going in after them, but concluded they could follow them better if they stayed put. More important, they wanted to avoid having to explain themselves when Herron read in their report that they had gone into the Hustler Club.

The party of seven stayed for two hours. The intel cops alternated taking catnaps. Finally, the group emerged. They got back into the limo and made their way back to the Pierre, where the two hitmen dropped off their passengers.

"And there they go," said Fitzsimmons. Back behind the wheel, the two mercs drove to a doorman building at 72nd and Second. McKenzie stayed behind the wheel while Hummel, with briefcase, went inside. Fifteen minutes later, he re-emerged with a passel of women – five blonds. Though the two cops had been on the job since the Irish breakfast, they were wide awake now.

"Is this what I think it is?" Gargiulio said.

"Take five hookers, add a case of Champagne and an ounce of coke and you've got a party fit for —"

"Some Saudi princes."

"Get some pictures of the girls, Tony."

"Oh, no worries," Gargiulio said, as the shutter clicked again and again and again.

Sure enough, the blond guests were ferried back to the Pierre. The mercs valet parked the limo and accompanied the women into the hotel.

"Chaperones?" asked Gargiulio.

"Or maybe sloppy seconds," said Fitzsimmons. "One thing's for sure: They're not planning anything first thing in the morning. The Saudis will be at it all night. I knew a guy who took his 20 and out. He caught a bunch of these jobs. You carry the briefcase with the cash – they pay as they go with big stacks of money; no American Express. You make sure no one hurts them, pick up the broads and make sure they go home happy. Bingo: you just made 25 grand. For the Saudis, coming here is like Vegas on crack: They get to do all the naughty shit they execute regular people for over there."

"So what is this, then?" asked Gargiulio. "A little moonlighting between assassinations?"

"You got it, buddy boy. Even killers have to pay the bills."

******

With Fitzsimmons and Gargiulio on top of the mercs, Ross concluded that it was safe to leave the safehouse. He took Tori to a cozy neighborhood restaurant in Greenwich Village. Then they went to Flynn's.

"Damn," Rudy muttered at the door after Tori had filed inside. Ross turned to him and beamed. Rudy high-fived.

Laura was there, but Sam, as usual, was involved in after-hours game production. Albert gasped when he approached Ross' spot at the bar and saw who he was with. He flirted mildly with Tori, just to get a rise out of Ross, and Tori pronounced his Irish accent cute. She agreed to a margarita – in honor of their special night in Tucson – but just one.

"If this goes down tomorrow and you're hung over," she told Ross, "I will kick you in a lethal strike point."

"You're so strict," he said.

Ross led her to the back of the bar to play Moose Hunt. Laura wandered over and joined the game.

"I haven't seen you in a week," she said. Motioning to Tori, she added, "I guess everything's good?"

"We're working a big case," Ross said. "We went over the wall tonight." Whispering, he added, "Everything's great."

"She's spectacular," Laura whispered back.

Ross shot the lights off Moose Hunt. "I'm never playing this again," said Laura. She steered Tori into a corner to talk.

Ross headed out front for a smoke.

"Did you kidnap her from Fashion Week?" Rudy asked. "Is she a model?"

Ross grinned. "Actually, she's my bodyguard."

"My hat's off to you, bro. Maybe it's just a big coincidence, but you don't seem like an asshole tonight."

"Rudy," Ross said, "it's not a coincidence."

Ross had finished his margarita and was well into a Rolling Rock when Laura returned Tori.

"She speaks highly of you," Tori said.

"We're old pals. Laura is the best. There are good people in here. But ... "

"But what?"

"For some reason it's not as exciting as it used to be."

"Hmm."

"Hmm. Exactly." He kissed her. "What do you say we get out of here?"

"Works for me." She kissed him. Albert appeared and cleared his throat loudly.

"Albert," Ross said, "don't make me shoot you."

They walked to the door and Ross froze as a redhead came in.

"Hi Ross," said Candy. Tori took Ross' hand.

"Hey," said Ross. Candy looked at Tori and back at Ross. Why now, he thought.

"I'm Tori."

"Hi, I'm Candy."

Ross pulled on Tori's hand. "I'd like to hang around and catch up, but we have to be up really early tomorrow," Ross said, and they quickly left the bar.

"Later, Ross," Rudy waved.

They walked halfway down the block before Tori said, "Well that must be the ex."

"*Very* ex," said Ross. "Awkward!"

"She seemed nice."

"Oh, but she's not. She's the opposite of nice," he said.

They caught a cab back to the safe house and headed directly for the roof,

"Much better," Ross said.

"What are the chances anyone else comes up in the next ten minutes?" Tori asked.

"No idea."

"Ooh," Tori said. "The risk of being caught."

"Are you proposing sex under the stars?"

Tori pulled him to her. "Do you have somewhere else you have to be?"

Chapter 24

The sounds of dawn in the city – the beeping of backward-creeping garbage trucks, the whooshing of taxis speeding down empty streets – jarred Ross awake. He didn't recall his neighborhood downtown as being this noisy, but it seemed like light years since he'd slept in his apartment.

Gray light seeped through the blinds. He found himself intertwined with the sleek warrior who was now his partner. Early morning was foreign territory for Ross but was quickly becoming something to savor. He contemplated Tori's rhythmic breathing and soaked up the sensation of her skin against his. He planted his nose in the nape of her neck, offering a silent prayer of thanks that there was no more talk of the sofa bed. He thought idly of strong, hot coffee, but nothing short of dragons and dinosaurs could make him budge from the bed they shared.

When she stirred, he craned his neck so he could see her open her eyes.

She found him gazing at her and smiled. "Hmm," she said softly. He kissed her eyes, her freckled nose, her lips.

******

Garbage trucks and speeding taxis were no match for Ironhead Hummel's snoring. McKenzie couldn't sleep. He checked for his weapon, an Army habit that had served him well, and saw his 9mm Colt, a short reach away on the night table, in the gray light.

He couldn't say he missed it. Waking up in a third-rate hotel was far superior than moments of combat sleep, ready to roll for his weapon and fire at the enemy. Certainly he had loved it, and he could still trigger an adrenaline surge just by replaying what he had lived through.

It was never the same after Tora Bora. They had fought through December 2001, yard by yard up the foothills, one firefight after another to get to the next pile of rocks. Hummel, a decorated sniper, picked off a Qaeda fighter every half hour. Waiting for reinforcements that never came, they never made the final push. The night before they pulled the plug, the enemy laid down a blanket of fire and made their break down the mountain. When the firing stopped, Hummel came down from his post panting. "I got him, Skip. I blew his head off."

"Who?" McKenzie asked. "Who'd you get?"

"Osama. I got him. Tall, skinny fucker. Scraggly beard. Saw him clear as day in the nightscope. Got him square in his melon. He's done."

They never recovered a body, and so the Army didn't buy it. McKenzie backed up Hummel's story and pushed it up the chain. They didn't like that. They were warned that what had happened in the Afghan mountains was classified and that they'd wind up in prison if they ever mentioned it again.

******

Dennis Bouton rode the No. 4 train, as instructed, to the 149th Street-Grand Concourse station. The two men with Yankees caps and Mets jackets were easy to find. In the SUV with tinted windows, he was blindfolded for the journey east.

Emilio Navarro wore a brown corduroy jacket with patches on the elbows.

"Welcome, Mr. Bouton. I apologize for the security procedures."

"Not at all," Bouton said. "I'd do the same."

They talked on the patio, as Navarro and Ross had four days earlier. Bouton accepted both coffee and a cigar. He hated to admit it, but Navarro was charming, an intelligent man, a good conversationalist. He had to remind himself that he was talking to a bloodthirsty thug who peddled enough poison to ruin millions of American dreams. He hated what he had come to do, but on balance, it was best for America. He learned long ago that war was a series of tradeoffs. If there wasn't collateral damage, you weren't doing your job.

"Mr. Navarro, I have a business proposition for you."

"I am always interested in business propositions, Mr. Bouton."

"How would you like a way to bring all the proceeds of your business back to your country undetected? Every last nickel?"

Navarro smiled. "Go on, Mr. Bouton."

******

Ross waited in the Impala on Lexington Avenue. "Coming out," Tori texted. McKenzie, 6 feet tall and thickly built, appeared first, followed by the mammoth Hummel. Ross recognized their bags. Checkout time. Tori, wearing a short black wig and oversized sunglasses, emerged and walked around the corner and out of sight. Without the disguise, the two hitmen surely would have recognized her from their skirmish on Jersey Street. Ross was disguised as the old man from his subway days.

The valet delivered a silver Nissan Pathfinder that McKenzie and Hummel loaded and drove off down 32nd Street. Ross pulled out onto Lex, made the left onto 32nd and picked up Tori. The SUV made the left to go north on Third Avenue. Ross lagged just long enough to stay comfortably behind but still make the light. He maneuvered behind a flying wedge of taxis as they followed the mercs up Third to 57th Street, where McKenzie, at the wheel, turned right.

"He's getting on the bridge," Ross said.

"Is that a good thing?" Tori said.

"It is if you like Queens."

"I hope it's better than New Jersey."

"No comparison."

She frowned. "Why do I get the feeling we're about to drive through nuclear waste?"

Traffic backed up on 57th, as usual, as cars stacked up for two blocks to turn left onto the ramp for the upper deck of the 59th Street Bridge.

"I'm getting hot all over for you as a brunette," he said.

"Keep it zipped, buster, we're on the job." They achieved another two feet. The driver in front, thinking better of getting caught in the middle of the intersection, hit the brakes sharply.

"If you don't crash, there's a little something in it for you," Tori said.

"Ooh, I love bribes," Ross said. "Particularly sexual favors."

"Yeah, *favor*, that's exactly it." Traffic oozed up the ramp, complicated by the New York merge, a counterintuitive technique that involved forming a third lane on the shoulder when two lanes were about to become one.

"What is wrong with people in this town?" asked Tori. "Was there a brain damage flu going around about a generation back?"

"Too much to see, and so little time," Ross said.

He grinned at his own joke and pulled her toward him in a deep kiss. A cabbie merging aggressively watched the old man making out with the young, attractive woman and shook his head sadly.

The Impala fought its way onto the bridge proper, landing three cars behind the Pathfinder. They exited at 21st Street and wound through the industrial streets of Long Island City.

"This is attractive," Tori said making a horrified expression.

"And I suppose every square inch of Denver is like Fifth Avenue?" Ross parried.

"Denver is a damn nice town."

"I wouldn't know. I've never been there."

"Well time's a-wastin'. You come to Denver and I'll show you around."

"OK." Ross looked at her. "Were you expecting me to argue with you?"

Tori studied the dreary landscape.

"What do they do in these buildings?" she pointed at the blocky brick facades, the grimmest of warehouse landscape, "boil bodies in acid?"

"Mostly, yeah. If they're not sacrificing virgins – blond virgins."

"You need to come to Colorado. You're like one of those bugs living under a rock. You may just like it out in the sunshine."

"What?" They drove down a block of grimy buildings, wind-driven trash and a burned hulk of a Ford. "And give up all this?"

The Pathfinder wound north through Queens, finally turning east onto Astoria Boulevard and into the tiny parking lot at the Kiwi Diner.

"Jeez," said Tori, "wasn't this where that dirty cop– "

"Yeah. These guys are cold-blooded."

They pulled up by a hydrant across the street. Ross examined the exterior of the diner where Margolis had had his last meal. "The most important meal in an assassin's day," Ross said.

After breakfast – pancakes for Hummel and an omelet for McKenzie, Tori, with the aid of binoculars, was quite certain – the deadly contractors wandered onto the Grand Central Parkway east toward Long Island – past Douglaston and Casa Colon.

"Where are they going?" Ross wondered. The Pathfinder kept plunging east on the winding Northern State Parkway. The landscape turned green, the edges of the parkway rimmed with woods and thick vegetation.

"This is more like it," Tori pronounced.

"Yeah, this is tremendous, if you like hay fever." Ross wondered if they were going to Montauk, another hundred miles away at the far tip of Long Island.

With Tori working the binoculars, Ross was able to keep far back. "He's getting over to the right," said Tori. "He's getting on this Meadowbrook Parkway."

"Where the fuck are they going?" They kept driving, now headed south toward the ocean. The Pathfinder made a series of lane changes to avoid a line of cars backed up at an exit for a giant shopping mall. Ross did the same. This parkway was also lushly landscaped and even more densely green at the edges. Finally they passed over a bridge and could see the beach – Jones Beach – and the Atlantic Ocean. The Pathfinder pulled into a deserted parking lot. Ross pulled behind some trees on the far side of the enormous lot.

"Unless they're getting picked up by a submarine, I don't think we need to worry where they're going."

"They've come to walk on the beach?" said Tori. "How cute!"

"Let's just sit on the truck here. We'll get made if we go on the beach."

They sat and listened to the waves crashing and the gulls shrieking. Tori reached out to stroke the back of Ross' head but erupted in hysterics. "I'm sorry. I can't make it with an old man in a parking lot."

Ross checked himself out in the rear view. "Yeah, old man Walton. I'm going to have to retire this disguise. Getting mugged is one thing, but losing out on car sex …"

Hours passed as the hired killers communed with the sea. Ross finally relented to Tori's begging to "go see that they didn't drown." They hadn't. She watched from the dunes as the big guy walked back and forth just to the dry side of the wash. He seemed to be collecting shells. The other one sat cross-legged in the sand, perfectly still, looking to sea. Tori returned to the Impala, answering Ross' inquiring raised eyebrows with a palms-up who-knows-what-these-nut-jobs-are-up-to.

Ross went for his own inspection and found the two ex-soldiers sitting side by side, at one with the ocean. He returned to the car. "If they're not done here soon," he told Tori, making a pained face, "we're gonna have to wait some more."

"These are the weirdest killers I've ever dealt with," Tori said.

"They're very sensitive killers."

"New-age killers!"

They had moved the car even farther away, but Tori was able to spot the nature boys when they finally emerged over the dunes. They walked directly to the Pathfinder and drove back toward the parkway. The mercs retraced their route up the Meadowbrook, but bounced over to the Long Island Expressway and headed west, back toward the city. There was no mistaking where they were headed when they exited at Little Neck Parkway for Douglaston.

They followed the Pathfinder north from the highway through the winding streets of the Queens neighborhood. The hitmen drove slowly, obeying all the traffic laws. At Northern Boulevard, they stopped for a long light as four lanes of dense traffic cruised by.

The neighborhood turned dramatically more expensive north of Northern Boulevard. Large attractive houses sat on small but well-tended, verdant properties.

A block from Colon's expanisve Tudor house, they could see the brake lights of the Pathfinder up ahead. Colon's street dead-ended at the edge of a bluff overlooking Little Neck Bay. The hitmen slipped on orange vests and unloaded shovels and picks. They opened a manhole and put out a worksite barrier and a couple of extra traffic cones for good measure. Anyone who drove down the street would have to come nearly to a stop to get by safely. A classic phony checkpoint used for assassination around the world.

"What's Colon drive?" Tori asked.

"Blue Lexus. Brand new."

"That's what I thought," she said, training the binoculars down the block behind them. "Like that?" The car slipped by them, headed toward the ambush.

"Fuck!" Ross floored it and quickly was on Colon's bumper. He hit the Impala's lights and siren. Ross frantically dug the Beretta out of the holster in the small of his back; Tori already held her Glock. They could see McKenzie and Hummel step forward, mildly confused by the commotion, but their pistols plainly by their sides. Colon stopped right by the fake worksite, as if he were hitting his mark. Ross lowered the windows and flung his door open. He could see Colon had dropped out of sight in his car.

"Police! Drop the gun!" Ross screamed. He had McKenzie on his side of the car. McKenzie took another peek inside the Lexus but couldn't see Colon. He fired three shots that were caught by the extra plating in the door of the Impala. Ross popped up and fired three in return. McKenzie dropped to the ground. Hummel got off a burst at Tori's side of the Impala, turned and jumped into the Pathfinder. Ross glanced through the Impala toward Tori. Where was she?

He ran around the front of the Impala to her side. She was down.

"Oh shit. Tori, oh shit. Where are you hit?" He

pulled off her wig to see where the wound was. "Where are you hit?"

"Go after him. I'm OK. I'll call it in." He tried to clear the blood with his hand. She was cut somewhere, but he saw no entrance wounds. "I'm fine!" she shouted. "Get after him!"

Ross sprinted toward the Lexus. Colon was cowering on the floor by the passenger seat. The keys were in the ignition. "Get the fuck out!" Ross yelled, waving his Beretta. "Out!"

Colon opened the door and rolled out. Ross threw the car into drive and floored it. He got a block when he realized that the street would dead-end as the finger of expensive real estate known as Little Neck met Long Island Sound. He could try to block the Pathfinder, but the SUV had the weight advantage and would have pounded the Lexus. He backed into a driveway and waited. Seconds later, the Pathfinder sped by; Ross pulled out behind it. They squeezed past the Impala toward the busier parts of Douglaston.

Ross was heartened to see a procession of squad cars and ambulances going the other way. They needn't hurry on McKenzie's account; Ross was sure he'd smoked him. He had a sick feeling having left Tori with some sort of a head wound.

The Pathfinder began to use the oncoming lane as it encountered traffic on the winding road. Panicked drivers were driving up on curbs as they spotted the two cars flying down the narrow streets. Hummel just made it back into his lane ahead of an oncoming car as it sped by the Long Island Rail Road crossing.

At Northern Boulevard, the Pathfinder flew against the light; eight cars pounded brakes. A Camry going east clipped the back of the Pathfinder and sent it into a 360. Hummel rode the spin and pulled out perfectly, continuing on his flight. Ross was able to pick his way across the debris field. Although the Impala had the brute power of a Police Interceptor, the Lexus was a major upgrade in handling.

Hummel made a series of squealing lefts and rights through the more modest neighborhoods of Little Neck. The Lexus cornered much better than the boxy SUV. Largely by driving in the oncoming lane, Hummel made his way back to the expressway. Passing six cars on the shoulder, he rocketed up the entrance ramp and into traffic, forcing a Hyundai to swerve left into a Ford Explorer. Ross avoided the spinning cars and stayed a car length behind the Pathfinder. The cars ahead seemed to sense the lunatic behind them and cleared a path. Ross checked his speed: 85 in tight traffic.

Hummel got right off at Lakeville Road, shot down the ramp, made a right on two wheels and a left to get onto the Northern State. Was he headed back to the beach? Would he evacuate by boat if it all went wrong? What the fuck were they looking at on the beach?

Ross could see smoke from the Pathfinder's tires on some of the sharper turns on the winding parkway. Hummel continued to push the speed barrier, slipping onto the grass on the left lane and jumping lanes often and more and more erratically. At Searingtown Road, three State Police cruisers joined the chase. As one came alongside the Pathfinder, Ross saw Hummel point his pistol out the window and fire. The trooper dropped back.

Near Roslyn Road, Ross saw an opening on the right and accelerated. The Lexus had plenty of power and closed the gap on the hulking Pathfinder. Hummel looked over and raised the gun.

As the vehicles approached a 90-degree turn, Ross saw that the police had closed the road ahead and erected a blockade of police cruisers and tow trucks. He hit the brakes a moment or two before Hummel did in the Pathfinder. The Lexus came to an abrupt but highly stable stop. The Pathfinder fought the sensation to stop, the forward momentum setting the rear end into independent motion. The SUV flipped and rolled. It slid several hundred feet on its roof until it crashed into a tow truck in a shower of glass and metal.

Chapter 25

Matt North walked into Lyle Rucker's outer office with a confident stride that did not betray the catastrophe that had just taken place in New York. Rucker's receptionist admired North's tailored blue suit, which hinted at the sculpted body beneath it.

"Mr. Rucker's in a conference," the receptionist said with wink, "but I'll let him know you're here." She disappeared behind the paneled door. A moment later she led three Aero Exploration executives out of the office of their founder, chairman and CEO. North walked in to find Rucker seated at the conference table.

"Hello, Matt." He motioned him to a chair at the table. He studied North's poker face. "It's bad, isn't it."

"Yes sir, I'm afraid it is." He paused to let Rucker absorb this information. "A couple of undercover detectives stopped our men before they could complete their assignment. Both of our men were killed."

Rucker looked at North for a long time. He got up and walked to the window, his 50th floor office suite affording a sweeping view of downtown Houston. He had worked long and hard and made millions for this view, and he was not about to let a bunch of Yankees in the White House get in his way.

"I need to meet with Catapano," he said finally. He turned to face North. "Make that happen, Matt."

"Yes sir." North popped up and left Rucker to stare out the window.

******

Ross found Tori in a room at Bellevue.

"Told you I was fine," she said. Herron was seated in a corner.

"There was *a lot* of blood," Ross said.

"Just a cut." She parted her hair to allow Ross to inspect her stitches. "He shot up the side-view mirror on my side and pieces got me on the scalp. Wasn't even the bullet. You get a cut like that roping a calf."

Ross laughed a little too hard, from the adrenaline of the day. "Well remind me never to go calf-roping with you."

"You wouldn't know which end to rope."

"Of course I would. It's the … which end?"

"I knew it."

Ross turned to Herron. "Colon is OK?"

"He's mad that you took his car, but the commissioner convinced him that in the scheme of things, he made out pretty good."

"What an asshole," Ross said. "I didn't put a scratch on that car. Nice brakes, by the way. Hummel didn't look so good when I last saw him."

"Dead as you can get," said Herron. "Hitting that truck upside down at 90 mph wasn't so good for his brain."

"Wonder who gets his shell collection," said Tori.

"I swear to God, I thought he had a boat waiting," said Ross. "Where the hell was he headed?"

"I think he was trying to outrun you," Herron said. "Once he lost you, he could get himself straightened out. Obviously he hadn't counted on the barricade."

"How about the other one?" Ross asked.

"You nailed McKenzie between the eyes," said Herron.

"Two for two," said Tori. "All that Moose Hunt paid off."

"But that means we're back at a dead end," Herron said. The three of them reflected on that for a moment.

"Did they have anything on them? Anything in their car?" Ross asked.

"Like a business card?" asked Tori. "Len Frasier, arranger of international conspiracies? That kind of thing?" Ross gave her a dirty look and mouthed *Len Frasier?*

"We know McKenzie's had a series of $9,000 wire transfers – five in the past five weeks. But we can only trace them to an account in the Caymans."

"Nice retainer," said Ross. "So we can rule out that they were acting on their own to rid the world of loudmouth exiles."

"I don't think these two had particularly strong political views," said Herron, "other than that they hated the Army brass."

"There's no lever to pull in the Caymans?" Tori asked.

"No," said Herron, "that's what makes those offshore banks so popular. It's where dirty money goes to hide."

Ross thought about that. Suddenly he remembered his talk with Emilio Navarro.

"I wonder," said Ross.

Herron and Tori looked at him inquisitively. Ross turned to Herron. "Which bank was it? Can you get me an account number? Anything to go on? I've got an idea."

******

Matt North had an inconspicuous office on the 32nd floor of the Aero Exploration building. His view, like Rucker's, was to the north and the cluster of Houston corporate skyline. He stared at the sky and the glass-and-steel towers. How had they failed? He had vetted his team carefully and now they were all dead – killed by a burnout of a transit cop, according to his moles in the NYPD. Who the hell was this guy? He wondered if Breslin the lawyer knew anyone who could make an annoying cop go away.

Whatever. There were a number of ways out of this tangle, as he learned in the Agency.

North dialed a number. A woman answered: "Pharmacology."

"I'd like to leave a message for Dr. Catterson."

"Go ahead, sir."

"Mr. Roberts would like to make an appointment."

"Thank you, sir. I'll pass on the message."

Five minutes later, Catapano called on North's cell phone.

"Hi, Matt."

"Thanks for calling, sir."

"I'm in L.A. Can you get him out here tomorrow?"

"Absolutely, sir."

"Heard you really stepped in it."

"That's fair to say."

＊＊＊＊＊＊

Ross checked Tori out of Bellevue and persuaded her, after prolonged discussion, to give her lacerated scalp a rest at their safe house.

"Do what you do when you're alone," he had told her.

"Worry about you."

"I've managed to stay alive in New York for 32 years."

"Yeah, but I've known you for only a week and you've been attacked and kidnapped."

"I'll be fine. Really. I studied my strike points."

He took off for Queens to play his ace in the hole.

Riding the subway for the first time since the meeting with Herron that changed his life, Ross made it to Rego Park in 30 minutes. He bounded up the steps at 63rd Drive and scanned the addresses on Queens Boulevard. Two blocks east, he walked into a bagel shop and easily found Luis: a Colombian with the physique of a weightlifter and an aura of menace.

"Ross, sit down," he said cheerfully, though he did not smile. "The egg bagels here are the best." Ross looked around and saw a Korean man behind the counter staring fearfully at the Colombian.

"What's up with him?" Ross asked.

"He doesn't like me."

"Why's that?"

"We disagreed about the dough."

He looked back at the bagel maker. His arms were folded and he was looking suspiciously at Ross.

"The boss said to give you whatever you want," said Luis. "So what do you want?"

"The Cayman Islands. I need to crack an account in a Cayman bank."

Luis took a bite from his egg bagel with cream cheese schmear. He shrugged and swallowed. "That's it?"

"You can do that?"

"Yeah. Whose money do you think those banks are full of?"

"What can't you do?"

"I don't know. We can do almost anything," Luis said with a sneer that was probably as close to a smile as he could manage.

Ross passed him the account information. "How long do you think it will take?"

"Not long. It's a phone call. They always return our calls promptly."

******

Luis dropped Ross off at Roosevelt Avenue to catch the E train back to Manhattan. Not wanting to ignore the bruising Colombian's advice, Ross had bought a dozen egg bagels. As he rode the subway, he wondered if Tori knew a schmear from a beer – or even had ever eaten a bagel.

The subway made him jumpy. He assessed the shoes, looked for strange bumps in clothing, watched for predators sizing up the crowd.

At Queens Plaza, a homeless man in his 50s entered the train. He wore flip-flops on bare, dirt-encrusted feet. His hair was matted and his face, like the rest of him, was unwashed for – how long? In New York police lingo he was a "bag of worms," a veritable rotting corpse still walking the streets.

The four other occupants of the long bench where Ross sat jumped to their feet and fled to the far end of the car. Ross was a second too slow to escape the stench of filth and decay. Fortunately, he had only two stops of mouth breathing before 53rd and Lex, where he could change to head downtown.

Above ground finally, he took a big gulp of fresh air. His cell phone beeped. It was a text from Luis. "Aero Exploration" was all it said.

Chapter 26

Ross and Tori found Sammy by the chess players in Washington Square Park. NYU professors, nerdy kids, Pakistani taxi drivers and homeless denizens of Greenwich Village gathered to play breakneck games on stone tables. They slammed down their moves – click! – and punch the clock that timed their turn – bang! Tori was fascinated.

"Safe and sound," Sammy said to Tori as he gestured toward Ross.

"I owe you an apology," she said. "I was concerned."

"Ah, don't worry about it. A face like that – how can I be mad?" Tori rolled her eyes. "Roscoe, you take her to meet mom yet?"

"Don't start, Sammy," Ross said. "I got your text. 'Meet me, *braciole*.' Who texts that?"

"And he's half Sicilian," Sammy said to Tori. "Can you believe this guy?"

"What's a brash-o?" asked Tori.

"It's – you know," Sammy bent his arm at the elbow to illustrate. "Like, 'Hey, meet me, dumb ass,'" said Sammy. "You know, something you tell a friend."

"I see," she said, not seeing at all. The wind

kicked up a grit storm in the park and they shut their eyes and put their heads down until it subsided. More people gathered to watch the players, or to wait their turn at the boards.

"So do you have something for us, or did you just get us down here for Italian lessons?" asked Ross. Click! Bang! went the chess players.

Sammy adjusted the skinny knot on his skinny tie.

"Here's what I know," he began. "See," he said to Tori, "I'm no bad guy."

"Yeah, you're a prince," she said. There was a roar from one of the chess tables as a man in a tweed jacket with elbow patches lost to a ragged man in a torn coat. The loser got up sadly and was replaced by a boy who looked about 10. Click. Bang.

"Your detective who got whacked," Sammy said. "What do you know about him?"

"Margolis?" said Ross. "He was a hell of a detective, but then he turned into a scumbag rogue cop."

"Yeah, that's pretty much it." Sammy's eyes darted around. "Did you know he and your jeweler grew up together in Brooklyn?"

"I heard that," said Ross. "Interesting, but what's that got to do with the price of tomato sauce?"

Sammy looked sideways at Tori. "Do you ever model? Cause I know a guy—"

"Sammy, cut the crap!" Tori sighed.

"OK. OK. One of the many clients of this rat-fuck Margolis" – he made a face of disgust; "the only thing worse than a cop is a *dirty* cop." He shook his head and continued. "One of his clients were the Colombian cartels. See where this is going?"

"I think so," said Tori.

"Jeweler pal, old buddy," he pantomimed the introductions, "meet my Colombian stone killer friends over here. Go make beautiful music together – and watch your ass."

"I'm missing something," said Ross.

"Yes, you are. Did he make this match out of the goodness of his heart? And it's debatable if the prick ever had one."

"I'm guessing 'no,'" said Tori.

"Very good guess," said Sammy. "Ever hear the name Matt North?"

Ross looked at Tori, who shrugged her shoulders. "We give up," he said.

"He's the guy Margolis put the gold laundry together for. Now here's where it really gets good. North's in town a few nights ago with one of his Colombian buddies who wanted to impress him, so his amigo takes him to this V.I.P. whorehouse in Queens. Run by the Colombians like a special candy store for their best business associates. The kid falls in love. Maybe he never had his pipe cleaned by a pro, who knows? Anyway, the *stugots* leaves her his fucking business card." He threw down an imaginary card for emphasis. "His *business card.*"

"Matt North, professional douche bag," said Ross.

"Wow," said Tori. "That must have been some blowjob." They both looked at her in surprise. "What?" she said indignantly.

"So where's the guy from?" asked Ross.

"He's from Houston. Works for some oil company called Aero Exploration."

Click. Bang.

******

Mayor Fernando Silva sat on a rust-colored sofa, dressed in black tie. Herron spotted his formal jacket on a hanger behind the oak door to his study in Gracie Mansion. Police Commissioner Jack Steele sat at the other end of the sofa and Herron took a chair next to the mayor. Silva massaged his face with both hands: After the hour he had cleared for the police officials, his marathon day would take him to a charity benefit at the Waldorf-

Astoria.

"From the beginning, Bill," the mayor said. "Let me have it."

"Yes, sir." Herron crossed his legs and thought of how to begin. The whoosh of traffic reminded him that the FDR Drive lay just beyond the grounds of the mansion. "The murder of the jeweler in the subway was carried out by three former Special Forces specialists – a Navy SEAL and two Green Berets. The SEAL was killed at the scene by our officer who happened to be wandering by. Pure luck. His investigation determined that the other two had been commissioned to assassinate the Venezuelan dissident Colon near his house in Douglaston."

"I've briefed the mayor on this," Steele said. "After Walton broke up the ambush."

Herron nodded and continued. "We tracked payments to these two – McKenzie and Hummel – from an offshore account. Walton's people, with reach into the banks, told us the source was Aero Exploration."

"Lyle Rucker's oil company," the mayor said.

"Yes," Herron said.

"Fuck," the mayor said. "How certain are we of these sources of Walton's?"

"It checks out," Steele said. "Our investigation in the Margolis case linked him to a guy named Matt North."

"Margolis was deep with the Colombians?" the mayor asked.

"He was deep with anybody with a buck," Steele said. "It appears if you came to town and needed some dirty work done, Margolis was the man to start with."

"North connects Margolis to Rucker?" the mayor asked.

"North works for Rucker, yes," Herron said. "He's on the Aero payroll. Former CIA in Colombia. About two years ago he found private enterprise more rewarding. The guy's no oilman. He's there for black

- 185 -

ops."

"So Rucker's answerable at least to conspiracy in the execution of a New York police detective."

Steele and Herron both nodded.

The mayor groaned. "So are these guys done here? Are there any other mercenaries ready to shoot up the subway? Any more assassination plots we need to worry about?"

"Not at the moment," Herron said. "But these people – North and Rucker – have been very determined. They hired highly trained talent to kill the jeweler and assassinate Colon."

"And there are a lot more people with their sort of training out there looking for work," Steele said.

The mayor clasped his hands behind his head and sat back. "What was so special about this jeweler?"

"For one, he grew up in Williamsburg with Margolis," said Steele, "which leads us to conclude that Margolis put him into the cash-to-gold money-washing scheme with the Colombians. The jeweler was otherwise clean as a whistle. And we've got indications this was a sanctioned operation – the FBI looked away."

The mayor scowled. "Washington needs a favor from the Colombians so they cook up a dark alliance. They need to make it all go away, so they reach outside for someone to clean up. I know this story." The mayor studied the ceiling. Herron and Steele exchanged a long look but said nothing.

"Your boy," the mayor told Herron, "the subway cop – he's pretty good."

"He's done very well. He saved us from toe-tagging a high-profile exile in a quiet Queens neighborhood. That's the 6 o'clock news for a week. I think this is a good fit for him. He had great instincts on the street before the — "

"The Ferguson case," Steele finished for him. "Wrong place, wrong time."

"Jack," the mayor asked, "what's the next move?"

"Well, sir, we would send Walton after North – he's got to answer for two murders – Shapiro and Margolis – and an assassination conspiracy. I can't imagine he would have gone ahead on this without Rucker's blessings. But Rucker is someone who lunches with the President. They've got to take care of their own." Steele smiled weakly. "That's where you come in, sir."

"Yes. Gunfight at the OK Corral." He looked carefully at Steele and then Herron. "Looks like I'll be going to Washington to make some noise."

******

Ross passed the lo mein.

"Why do you suppose Americans never learned to put food in paper cartons?" asked Tori. The lights of the city illuminated their Chinese takeout picnic on the roof of their hideaway building.

"You ask all the right questions," Ross said. "Tell me liver and onions wouldn't taste better in a takeout carton."

"Or Rocky Mountain oysters."

"What kind of oysters?"

Tori held a noodle high overheard and dangled it into her mouth. "Not really oysters. It's a Colorado thing. You take a bull's testicles and — "

"Whoa. Hold it right there." He held up a carton crammed with white rice. "For starters, I don't think a bull nut would fit into one of these."

"Oh no, they slice them before they go into the batter." She made a chopping motion with her left hand.

"Remind me to avoid Colorado." Ross reached for the carton of General Tso's chicken and plucked out a nugget with chopsticks. He held it up to inspect it in the shadowy light of the rooftop. "Now everything looks like testicles. Thanks a lot." He tried to light a cigarette, but the breeze cutting across the sky snuffed his lighter. "Hey, let's move it downstairs," he said. "I'm freezing my oysters off."

Tori, her gaze locked on a building across town, was lost in thought.

******

They made their preparations for Houston. Neither of them had ever been there, so they needed to familiarize themselves with the streets and the route between the airfield where a government plane would wait while Matt North was hauled in.

North's profile from the Intel analysts was of a slick and dangerous character. He'd undergone Ranger training while with the Agency and landed in Colombia, in the thick of the war on drugs. The Agency liked him. He'd developed a reputation as methodical and vicious. He could play the cartels off one another and stay alive in the process. They respected his ability to work both sides of the street.

But suddenly, North jumped to the private sector. Now he had an anonymous office in Lyle Rucker's office tower and a vague job description of special projects manager. A New York State Supreme Court justice had been persuaded that among North's special projects was the assassination of Detective Ronald Margolis. Ross was bringing an arrest warrant to Houston.

"So after North falls, then what?" Tori asked. She brushed hair out of her eyes.

"Then," Ross began, moving next to Tori on the floor, "the Manhattan DA gets North to flip. And we reel in the big fishies." He wrapped his arms around her and kissed her neck. Tori wrestled him to the floor and in minutes their clothes were scattered around the tiny living room.

They tumbled into bed. Tori was a formidable partner, athletic and strong. Their unions were not a delicate affair. For Ross, their lovemaking was a form of erotic cross training – a full body workout – ending in the most blissful exhaustion.

Afterward, they lay panting and sweaty.

"I'd love to have a cigarette, right here in bed. But you'd kill me."

"That's right," said Tori. "Wouldn't need a bullet. I'd just give your skinny little neck a twist." She demonstrated in the air. "Or I could kick you in the temple again."

"Nearly worked the first time." Their breathing was returning to normal.

"Tell me something," Tori said.

"Anything. Secret codes, combinations to safes. Whatever you need, Mata Hari."

"Why do you stay in this town? There must be horrible memories wherever you go."

"Can I smoke if I answer your questions?"

"Stop it. Answer the question."

Ross exhaled dramatically. "I have a younger brother. I'm five years older. Mom moved back upstate with him when he was 17, to get him out of the projects. Smart kid. Got into SUNY Binghamton, then moved out west. He's in a little town in the Cascades in Oregon."

"So, why didn't you go?"

He looked at her. Lying beside her seemed to fix all the broken things inside him.

"I had business to do here," he said at last. "Whenever I arrest some creep messing with people trying to live a decent life it helps me make sense of – you know – my father." Tori took his hand.

"Tell me about your family," Ross said. "Wait, let me guess: Youngest of five. Four older brothers. Tomboy, toughest of the bunch."

She laughed. "Oldest of four girls. You suck at this. My dad was a dentist and mom stayed at home. We were as normal as they come. Just taller than the average suburban white people. Dad's six-foot-six. Viking blood, I guess."

"Bucktooth and gangly until you hit puberty?"

"No! What have you been reading?" She socked him on the arm. "I did hit my full height at 15. That was awkward. But I never hunched or stooped. I could feel grown men looking at me, but I knew I could kick their asses, so who cared?"

"God you're beautiful," he said as he reached for her.

******

Ross was jolted from sleep by squealing brakes. Now he was wide awake, alone with middle-of-the-night thoughts: Was he in over his head in a world of trained killers and spies? Would he disappoint Tori? Herron?

Tori was deep asleep. Ross breathed in her scent and admired her lanky form, barely distinguishable in the dark. He craved a cigarette, but didn't want to dress to go up on the roof. He padded out of the bedroom, through the kitchen and into the living room.

Ross opened the window in the living room and stood naked and shivering. His eyes had adjusted to the shadows, and he found his cigarettes on the coffee table. Finding his lighter in the dark was more of a challenge.

The hospital entrance was quiet for a change. Ross' eyes settled on a car parked a few doors down the street. It was a silver Lexus.

He dropped the cigarette when the front door crashed open.

Ross' Beretta was on the night table in the bedroom. He picked up a pole lamp and in three quick strides met the first one through the door, thrusting the lamp like a lance.

The intruders' eyes had not adjusted to the dark in the apartment. Ross swung at another and put him down. The third one had a pistol in his hand, and Ross grabbed for it.

"Ross! Get down!" Tori shouted from the bedroom door. He took the third intruder down with him, as the first two got up from the floor. The lights flashed on. Tori, stark naked, was on one knee, holding the Beretta in combat stance. With her eyes all but closed against the light, she squeezed off six gut-level shots in a short arc around the door. The other two cried out and toppled. Ross had his right hand on the wrist gripping the gun and was feeding punches with his left. The intruder grabbed a fistful of hair.

Tori stood over them and held the Beretta an inch from the intruder's left eye. "Give me an excuse, Benny," she said. "I would love to blow your eye out the back of your fucking head."

Chapter 27

Lyle Rucker's mood darkened the minute his jet touched down in Van Nuys. He hated Los Angeles and its bad traffic, fake breasts and worship of pretension. Scratch the surface and no one was who they said they were.

Rucker tried to control his emotions in the car that Catapano had sent to take him to their meeting. The president's counselor used a Wilshire Boulevard law office as his base of operations when he was in town. Rucker wasn't in the habit of prostrating himself, but the prize was so juicy there wasn't much he wasn't willing to try short of putting Debbie on the street.

Adding to his sour disposition was the inescapable realization that North had failed him. He'd had such high hopes for him. He had come so highly recommended. North was disciplined, smart and unafraid to be ruthless. His connections – the intel community, Colombian cartels, Washington – were valuable. And yet, he had allowed the Marquez cartel to play him for the fool. Then the debacle with the mercs in New York.

He'd thought North could succeed him one day. Polished and trim, youthful and energetic, he'd already made an impression on a lot of the right people in Houston. Even Debbie seemed to like him. But Matt North would have to go.

Rucker was highly unimpressed with the building. This was where the right hand to the President received one of his biggest financial backers? He entered the lobby alone, feeling like a gunslinger, and was greeted warmly by a shapely redhead who escorted him past security and into a fast elevator to the 36th floor offices of Snow Taylor & Fleet. Her name was Rachel and she did her job well, clasping Rucker on the forearm to emphasis key aspects of her tour of the offices. She stayed close enough to keep her perfume circulating in the oilman's olfactory receptors.

Rucker was trying to memorize her green eyes when she finally led him to the suite where Catapano was receiving visitors. The sumbitch is good, he thought, realizing he'd been worked as surely as if someone had slipped him Ecstasy.

"Lyle, great to see you, sir," Catapano enthused, as he extended his hand. "How's Debbie?" His hair was an unkempt mop, but he wore an exquisitely tailored gray sport jacket over a navy blue turtleneck.

"Marvelous," he said. "Thanks for taking the time, Tom." They sat in high-backed leather chairs grouped around a glass table by the window. The view was of generic LA sprawl. Amateur hour.

"The President sends his best," Catapano said.

"I appreciate that."

"So what is it I can help you with, Lyle?"

Rucker leaned closer. "Are we speaking freely here?"

"Absolutely." Catapano beamed. "The lamps here are just lamps – no listening devices. The White House? Different story entirely. And, of course, we have to be careful about what's said in front of the President. You understand."

"Well I certainly do now," Rucker said and smiled in an exaggerated way. He looked out the window but could find no inspiration in this view. "I want to go back to Square One with you boys. Maracaibo is a gusher, and

I need to be working there. Now, we've tried a couple of things to get this thing moving but we've failed. I admit that. But we're willing to work more closely with ya'll. And I don't need to remind you how willing to help we've been in the past."

"You sure don't."

"No. You boys say write a check and I say how much."

Catapano smiled in a way that did not convey amusement.

"Tom, I'm shaking up my staff and I'm going to find the right man to get this moving forward again."

Catapano folded his hands in his lap and hung his head. Finally, he looked up. The smile was gone. "It's over Lyle."

"What?"

"You know when wells catch fire and shoot geysers of flames into the sky?" Rucker felt acid flare in his stomach. "That's what we've got here. This is a bad, bad situation. The police are all over the mess in New York. This operation is way too hot. *You're* way too hot."

"What are you telling me?"

"We have to walk away from you, Lyle. I'm sorry."

"Sorry?" Rucker fought the urge to throw the curly-headed twit 36 floors to the street below. "You're sorry? Do you know how much money I've put out for you all? Do you know how much dirty work I've done on this thing? No, *I'm* sorry. You don't walk away from me."

"Lyle, at this moment a team of Treasury agents and S.E.C. lawyers are carrying your financial records out of the Aero Building. You shouldn't be sitting here talking to me. You need to go find your lawyers."

******

Ross hadn't talked to his mother for a couple of

weeks. So much had changed since then. She called his cell phone while he was at his apartment picking up some fresh clothes.

"Sorry I haven't called, Ma. A lot's been going on."

"Um, I have some news myself, Rossy." He waited for her to continue. It sounded like bad news. "The parole board met last week." Ross felt his stomach tense. "They're letting him out."

Ross wasn't sure he'd heard right. He hoped he hadn't.

"What?"

"I said they're letting him out. I was at the hearing. They all —"

"Why didn't you tell me?"

"I didn't want you going up there. They'd turned him down once. I didn't think —"

"You should have told me, Ma. Maybe I could have —"

"They all said how much he had rehabilitated himself. All these prison officials. He got a college degree. He counsels the convicts how to kick drugs."

He did the math. Nineteen going in meant he was 42 now. Lots of time to enjoy life. His father was dead forever.

"Ross?"

"Yeah. OK, it's going to be OK, Ma."

"Ross."

"Yeah, Ma."

"Don't do anything stupid."

******

Rachel did not escort Rucker out in a cloud of perfume. He charged out of the law office in a red rage.

His car appeared as he emerged from the lobby. Out of a cloud of anger emerged the realization that some pissant cop in New York had ruined his plans. He would enjoy getting even with the little prick, once he had replaced North with someone who was competent.

As he cooled off, the logical part of his mind began to evaluate what Catapano had told him about the S.E.C. It wouldn't be very hard for the feds to take a pile of documents and construct some kind of cock-and-bull case no jury could ever understand. They would only see a well-dressed man who had made a lot of money. No mercy from the have-nots.

He could pack up Debbie and head for Sao Tome, the island nation off the Atlantic Coast of North Africa. There was no extradition to the United States. There was even some oil there. He had plenty of cash tucked away in offshore accounts. The Treasury Department could kiss his Texas ass.

He tried on visions of life in a seaside villa. Debbie loved the beach. But by the time his jet had lifted off from wretched Los Angeles, his thoughts turned to growing up poor. He never ran from ridicule, from chants of "trailer trash"; he fought back, even when winning was unlikely. He was never afraid of a bloody nose. He just couldn't turn and run. It was against his nature.

Rucker spent the flight back to Houston fielding panicked calls from his executives. He listened carefully, told them to heed his legal people and assured them that all was well. He was unusually calm. This, after all, was the management acumen that had allowed him to build an international business. On landing, he instructed his driver to take him home.

Home was an antebellum mansion on 27 acres that Rucker had bought from a Texaco heir. When his car passed through the gates, he knew there was no way he would leave this behind. Never.

He found Debbie in the bedroom. She was watching CNN and hurriedly finishing a phone call. She saw Rucker and hung up. "I heard. My God, Ly, what's happening?" She looked upset, but not panicked. Debbie was always calm in a storm.

"I'm all over this, darlin'. My lawyers will eat them for breakfast." He threw his suit coat on a chair and took off his tie.

"Can I fix you a drink? God, you must need one."

"You might say that. The old Scotch, no ice. Thank you, darlin'."

Rucker rounded up his legal team and arranged for an emergency meeting that night. His experience had been that the sooner you showed your guns, the sooner the other side wanted to compromise. He was beginning to feel back in control, and his thoughts came around again to Maracaibo and the bounty his company would find there. He wasn't letting go of that.

He was sitting in an armchair in the bedroom, sipping his second Scotch. Debbie flipped channels on the TV, finally settling on a *Law & Order* rerun.

A little pinch.

That's what they always said when they gave you a flu shot: "You'll feel a little pinch." He felt a little pinch on the side of his neck.

He turned to see Matt North.

"Hello, Mr. Rucker." North had to go. What was he doing here, in his bedroom?

"I've just injected your jugular with curare. It's really cool stuff. The Indians in the Amazon just love it. They rub it on their arrowheads to bring down game. In a moment, you'll be paralyzed and find it difficult to breathe." Rucker tumbled out of the chair.

"There you go." North put him back in the chair. "Debbie dear, the gun?"

Debbie walked over to Rucker's side of the bed and pulled a pistol – Rucker's pistol – from his night table. She presented it to North as he put on latex gloves. He put the gun in Rucker's right hand.

"Wait!" Debbie yelled. "He's a lefty."

"Oops. *Excellent* catch." North switched the gun to Rucker's left hand and placed his limp index finger on the trigger.

"So long, Mr. Rucker."

Chapter 28

Firing blindly, Tori had shot two of the intruders in the abdomen. When the light had flicked on, one of the attackers was turned sideways. He was essentially fine; the bullet had passed just under the skin and out without even penetrating the abdominal cavity. The other one had turned fully toward Tori. This would be the last mistake he would ever make. The bullet hit his pelvic bone, sending bone splinters and bullet fragments into his liver and other essential organs and knifing through his inferior vena cava. He was long dead by the time EMTs showed up.

Tori instantly recognized the third man – Benny Chen, one of the counterfeiters from Seattle. Chen's brother Pete had been the one Tori had caught up with after the murder of her Treasury agent partner. Benny Chen and his assassins had tracked Tori to New York and had even followed them halfway to Philadelphia in a silver Lexus.

They put off the trip to Houston for a day to move into a new safe house, this one on 28th Street near Third Avenue. Ross had insisted it have roof access. After they'd gotten settled, they went up to check it out. There was an outstanding view of the Empire State Building, six blocks north and several avenues west.

"I told you I needed you to watch my back," Tori

told Ross.

"We owe our lives to some crazy taxi driver," said Ross. "If he hadn't hit the brakes so hard and woken me up, they would have killed us both in bed. Not a bad way to go, but still … "

"So you're not so useless after all."

"I'm thinking I'm more useful every day."

Tori launched into her kata, spinning kicks and firing volleys of punches. "I think I like this rooftop even better."

"Don't hurt it," Ross said, as Tori took two giant steps, leaped and kicked in the air.

She stopped and looked at Ross. "I knew they were coming for me. Occupational hazard. Get used to it, spy man."

******

Debbie Rucker, newly widowed, dug her nails into Matt North's back and moaned. She put her tongue in his ear and whispered: "I want you to rip them." He reached down and tore off her panties.

"You're so young and strong," she panted. "Fuck me, Matt. Fuck me hard."

North's eyes shut in rapture. He moved furiously over her, running his hands over her bronzed skin. The most desirable woman in Texas. The wife of a billionaire. Until moments ago.

"We did it, Matt," she said. "I want you. I want you to fuck me." She wrapped her legs around him. North grabbed a fistful of golden hair and locked his mouth onto hers.

Afterward, North lay on his side, his arm propping his head.

"We did it, Deb." He grinned. "The old man was a pushover."

"Stay cool, Matt. We're not there yet." She pulled the sheet up to her chin and lay still, trying to compose for the next stage.

North shook his head. "We've waited so long for this day and it's here." He reached under the sheet to stroke her breast. "It's here, Deb. The old man was a pushover. All that tough talk and he folded like a flower." He shook his head. "No more kissing his ass. No more kissing *anybody*'s ass. God, if I had to do much more of that I was gonna kill somebody." He laughed at his own joke.

Debbie nodded imperceptibly, trying to get into character.

"You're brilliant, Deb. And beautiful," North said. "Would you say you're more brilliant or more beautiful?" He tilted his head to ponder that. "Well, whatever; you're mine. And I love you."

Debbie pushed his hand away. "You'd better get out of here. I have a call to make."

North dressed quickly and left. She tidied up the guest room where they had made love and called 911. She was proud of her performance as the horrified wife who had found the body of her husband. Lyle Rucker still lay in their master bedroom with a bullet wound in his head.

She found the disposable cell phone she'd bought a week ago and made a second call.

"Pharmacology."

"I'd like to leave a message for Dr. Catterson," said Debbie Rucker.

"Go ahead, ma'am."

"Please tell him the cake is done. It came out just perfectly. And I'm going to bake another tomorrow."

"Thank you, ma'am. I'll give him the message."

******

Ross and Tori flew to Houston to snap cuffs on Matt North for arranging the murders of Yehuda Shapiro and Ron Margolis and the assassination attempt on Eduardo Colon. When the clandestine commuter plane landed at Teterboro, there were already passengers aboard – a slender man about Ross' age, casually dressed, and a dark-haired woman about Tori's age and approximate physical dimensions, dressed down to de-accentuate model-like features.

Ross and Tori moved to the back of the plane, studying their twins along the way. "What is this?" Ross whispered as they settled in and buckled up. "The fucking Twilight Zone?"

"You just never looked under the rock," Tori whispered back. "There are a lot of us bugs under there."

"I think I'm looking at us a week ago."

"He doesn't look quite as confused as you did," she said.

Ross and Tori donned headphones and went to sleep.

"Are you gonna live?" Tori asked. "Is anybody home?" They were in the subway. Monte, the Brooklyn mugger was slamming Ross' head into the platform. Crack! Crack! It didn't hurt, but he knew that the punishment was creating a widening pool of blood. The sound was sickening. "Are you gonna live?"

Ross awoke with a knot in his stomach and an odd sense of dread. Tori was sleeping peacefully. He could hear muffled techno Indian music from her headphones. Funny, to be in love with a killing machine.

******

Tori's plan was simple: Get into North's house and grab him when he got home. Herron had obtained warrants: North would be dealt with by the courts.

North lived in a townhouse in an attractive neighborhood east of Memorial Park. They went around back and Tori produced a gizmo that looked like a TV remote control. "This will search frequencies until—" the garage door opened – "until that happens."

They entered and Ross found the button inside to

close the door behind them. A door led to a flight of stairs that they followed into the living room. As Ross emerged from the stairs, a large form hurled itself at him from the right. He heard Tori race up the rest of the stairs and emit a battle shriek directed at someone else. Ross rolled on the floor with his attacker, who had a pronounced weight advantage. The thug tried a punch from short distance that Ross blocked. Ross headbutted and caught him in nose. The attacker sniffed the blood back and shifted his grip to Ross' adam's apple, pressing with a thumb. Ross whipped his chin down to block, wishing he had worked in the gym half as much as he had boozed and smoked at Flynn's.

Ross heard pottery breaking (lamps?) and the thud of a heavy body. It sounded like Tori was dribbling her opponent on the way to a layup. He wished she'd finish soon, while he could still hold off his attacker's attempts to push his windpipe out the back of his neck.

The man lost his grip and he reapplied it to Ross' mouth. Ross found a finger and part of his hand with his teeth and bit down as hard as he could. The man shrieked as Ross tasted blood and bits of skin and flesh.

"OK, cowboy." Tori had a huge pistol pressed against the man's temple. If she pulled the trigger, it would take Ross a week to rinse the man's brains out of his hair.

"You win," he said, hyperventilating. "Letting go." He unpeeled himself from Ross.

"What the …" said Ross. It was Mateo, George Rivera's expressionless sidekick from the World Famous Agave Lounge. Ross found the other man in a corner of the room. He knew him, too. The Little Scorpion had indeed come back to sting him. Ross dragged George Rivera, groggy from Tori's thrashing, next to Mateo. He cuffed them both.

"I need some answers really fucking fast. Like what the fuck are you doing here?"

Rivera and Mateo looked at each other. Neither

spoke.

"Here's the deal." Ross said. "I don't know if you're aware of who lives here, but he's a stone killer. So if I leave you morons sitting here handcuffed together like the retards you are, he's probably going to torture you until you tell him whatever it is you think he wants to know and then he'll shoot you each once in the head, so as not to waste bullets on dumb fucks like you. So who wants to go first now?"

Rivera was starting to come around. "This is Matt North's place. I know," he said, stretching his neck to try to get some feeling back in his spinal cord.

"Now that's a start," said Tori. "Were you following us, or did someone send you here?"

Mateo tilted his head back to try to stop his nose from bleeding. Ross found a paper towel and wadded two pieces to plug the leak.

"We came to kill him, because he killed my friend," Rivera said. Ross and Tori exchanged puzzled looks.

"Who's your friend?" Tori asked.

"A man named Rucker. Lyle Rucker. A very important man." Ross caught Tori in his peripheral vision as she did the same.

"I know Rucker," Ross said.

"Good," Rivera sneered. "That makes two of us."

"How do you know Rucker's dead?" Tori asked.

"I got a call."

"Start from the fucking beginning, George," Ross said.

Rivera stared into a far corner of the room. "Are you going to arrest us?" he asked.

"That depends," said Ross. "We were here to arrest North. He's a killer. We may be on the same side here, George. Just tell me the story, before he gets home. How long have you known Rucker?"

Rivera looked like he was trying to do the math. "A long time," he said finally. "Probably, mid-'70s, I'd say. Some of my business involved oil that was, ah, *borrowed* from the pipelines the government runs in Mexico. Rucker took it off my hands at a nice price. We did a lot of business. He never cheated me. He was honorable. About two years ago, he told me he had hired this North. He said he was shrewd and dangerous. He paid me a retainer. If I were to get a call from one of his people to say that he was gone – dead – I was to kill North."

"And you got the call," said Tori.

"Yes," he said. "Yesterday. A woman called. A young woman. She said she was calling to tell me that Rucker had been murdered by Matt North."

******

Tori spotted North's BMW as it turned into the alley and paused for the garage door to open. "He's in," she said. They sat halfway down the block in their rented car – Ross had insisted on an Impala. His throat was still raw from Mateo's murder attempt, and Ross could still taste shreds of his hand.

"This is clean," Tori said.

"Works for me," Ross said.

"He'd only take the fall anyway," Tori said. "You wouldn't get a word out of him."

Chapter 29

Ross checked his watch for what must have been the fifteenth time.

"How long should it take those guys to shoot this dude?" he asked.

"Who knows," said Tori. "Maybe it's a Tucson thing. A ritual. Like a bullfight."

"Or maybe they're getting him to talk." They locked eyes.

"OK," Ross said, "We're going back in."

They walked back to the townhouse. "I guess we have no choice," Tori said as she pressed her garage door zapper. The door began to open, noisily.

They entered the garage and pulled their pistols. Ross flung open the door. The stairs were clear, and he made his way up. Tori followed closely. Ross slowly padded up the carpeted steps to the living room where he had been jumped by Mateo not long before. He thought he heard heavy breathing. He peered carefully around the wall separating the stairs from the living room.

"You must be Ross!" said Matt North. "Come in and join the fun. And please bring your pretty blond partner I've heard so much about." North held an Uzi. Behind him sat George Rivera and Mateo, bound to chairs. They were gagged and bleeding and had ugly purple bruises on their faces. On the floor beneath them was a plastic tarp.

"Toss the gun here, please," North instructed Ross, who complied. Tori followed him into the room. "Oh my my my, you *are* gorgeous," he said. "So often people over-estimate beauty. And old George here, I didn't figure he had very high standards."

Tori looked him over.

"I've heard you're quite talented in the martial arts," said North, "but I've got the Uzi." He held it up for all to see better. "Isn't it a beauty? The original Uzi sub machine gun. Used to belong to Pablo Escobar – I'm not making this up! This thing is priceless!" Ross and Tori exchanged what-an-asshole glances.

"Your gun over her, sweetheart," North said. She slid her Glock across the floor. "That's a girl. You two have a seat over there, please." He directed Tori and Ross to a sofa by the wall. He took a seat opposite them, in front of an imposing wooden coffee table. "Sorry, but I ran out of rope on these two characters. You'll just have to behave yourself.

"Now, what no one seems to know – well, I guess Ross here knows – but neither George nor Mateo knows your name?" He looked expectedly at Tori, who said nothing. "I'm Matt and you're … "

"Tori," she said, with considerable irritation.

"Wow," said North "I *love* that name. Amazing woman like you, it just wouldn't do to have an ordinary name like Mary or Barbara. Tori – that's just lovely.

"Now, I understand that you and Ross are here to arrest me? Is that right?"

"You're under arrest for the murder of Detective Ronald Margolis," Ross began. "You have the right to remain silent—"

North laughed hysterically. "I love the sense of humor on this guy," he said to Tori. "He must keep you in stitches!" He turned to Ross. "You think you're Mr. Genius Cop, stopping me at every turn – shot Tony Bozzo in the subway, saved Eduardo Colon from getting whacked. Well guess what? It doesn't matter. You were wasting your time, cause I've got it all now! Couldn't have worked out any better! Rucker's dead and his wife gets his oil company. And guess who's fucking his wife?" His prisoners looked at him silently.

"Nobody got the answer? Come on, it's not a hard question."

"I'd say you," said Ross, "but I'm not sure anyone would lend you their dick to do it."

North exhaled sharply. He looked at Tori and said, "Don't you find New Yorkers to be crude?"

"Why don't you put down the Uzi, pretty boy," Tori said. "Let's you and me settle this."

North screwed up his face as if in deep thought. "Um, no thanks."

"Since we're chatting so nicely here," Ross said, "do you think Rucker's betters are going to let you walk away after screwing up, let's see," now Ross made a thinking face, "the Shapiro hit, the attack on me, the Colon hit. You're oh-for-three, Matty boy."

"Oh, this is where I explain everything nice and neat for you?" North answered. "I don't think so, cop."

North composed himself and continued. "So let's see: George and Mateo are here to *kill* me," he looked their way and shook his head disapprovingly, "and you two are here to arrest me. Well, hmm, I don't think I want to be killed *or* arrested. So I guess I'm going to have to kill all ya'll instead." Ross' eyes darted around the room. He stole a glance at Tori. She, too, was surveying the area.

North scrunched up his face as if in deep thought. "Now if I shot all four of you with the Uzi, I'd never finish cleaning up the blood and brains and bullet holes. So." He got up and backpedaled behind the kitchen counter at the opposite end of the room. "That's why we have this cute little .22." He held up a pistol to show everyone. "Makes just a teeny tiny hole, but it gets the job done."

"Don't tell me," Ross interrupted, "used to belong to John Wilkes Booth."

North smiled and said to Tori, "I like this guy! He can joke at his own execution. Now *that's* what I call a sense of humor. These guys," he pointed at Rivera and Mateo, both expressionless, "you hardly know they're alive."

"George" he looked at Rivera, who looked back wearily. "Age before beauty, I'm afraid. Nothing personal, guys, but I do want to spend some alone time with Tori. You understand."

Ross caught Tori's eye and glanced downward. She looked down and back at Ross.

North held the Uzi in his right hand, pointed at Tori and Ross. He extended his left hand with the .22. Rivera still looked perfectly at peace. Ross wondered just how many times someone had pointed a gun at his face.

"Seeya, George old buddy."

Tori and Ross lunged at the coffee table, picked up their end of it and rammed it at North. The .22 fired into the ceiling; the Uzi slid across the floor. Tori dived for the Uzi. North was stunned, but still held the .22. He pointed it at Ross but couldn't get a shot off before Ross brought the corner of the table down on North's head with the intent of putting his smirk deep into the ground.

Tori walked over with the Uzi. Ross drew the table away from what remained of North. Rivera and Mateo craned to inspect what was left of his head. Tori bent down and tried to find a pulse.

"That's all, folks," she said, shaking her head.

They freed Rivera and Mateo, and the four of them wiped down what they had touched in the house. Rivera and Mateo cleaned the blood off their faces and helped themselves to bandages from North's bathroom.

"Look me up when you're in Tucson," Rivera said as he shook Ross' hand. "Drinks are on me at the Agave."

"That makes it all worthwhile," Ross said.

Wordlessly, Mateo shook Ross' hand and they

went on their way.

North lay in a widening pool of blood. It would be a closed-coffin service.

Chapter 30

Congressman Jerry Hartman was waiting when Mayor Silva returned to his office. Hartman – tall, bald and paunchy – had an uncanny resemblance to Ed Koch and always caused the long-timers around City Hall to do a double take. Hartman was an early supporter of Mayor Silva and was a welcome visitor.

"What can you tell me about this mess, Jerry?"

"Hard to say, Mr. Mayor. As you know, I can't disclose what comes out in the briefings to the Intel Committee. But as your friend, I can give you some insight."

"I hear you. We never spoke. But I'm all ears."

Hartman nervously scratched his bald scalp. "This is definitely an outsourced White House deal. I don't know that they planned on all the cowboy work in New York, but that may have been outside their oversight. This cast of characters — it's interesting. This fellow Rucker—"

"Who committed suicide."

"Yes. Apparently. He was in the White House just about 10 days ago. Was having a quiet lunch with the President when Morgan leaves suddenly and Dennis Bouton – a military assistant on the National Security Council staff – got in a tremendous row with him. They essentially tossed Rucker out of the White House."

"That's bizarre. How did you find out about that?"

"Ah, Washington. The first order of business is to snoop. Knowledge is power. The Secret Service cashes this goody in for something and it gets traded like an old baseball card on eBay. Before you know it, I'm here telling you."

"I understand. Please, continue."

"Now Rucker is an oilman, and oilmen want oil. Clear and simple. He was also a big contributor to Morgan's campaign, so you can reasonably think he was expecting to see some return on his investment."

"That's the way it usually works," said the Mayor.

"Right. Rucker had an aide named Matt North – you know all about him. Hired out of the Agency, spent time in Colombia, the drug war, met all the players etc. etc. Now why does a guy like Rucker need someone like North?"

"Venezuela."

"Very good." Hartman smiled. "You really don't need me at all."

"We can guess, Jerry, but what do you *know*?"

Hartman smiled again. "As you know, we get 'briefings' – the Agency, Andrea Hopkins and her people, NSA, all of them. But they're more valuable from the aspect of what they won't talk about. What's clear is there's an awful lot of energy being expended in the White House to knock out Gallegos."

"Can't really blame them; he's a creep."

"Yes, he is an asshole, no doubt. But we can't be too heavy handed down there cause every country in South America is sensitive to anything that looks like U.S. interventionism."

"They've seen enough of that over the years."

"Exactly. And the memories aren't pleasant. We helped give them Pinochet in Chile and the Dirty War in Argentina. But the Agency and the National Security staff in the White House, with a sharp stick and some string, are trying to start a fire without any matches. We certainly won't allow overt funding of covert ops."

"So if they make a deal with an oil guy and say start some shit and it will be worth your while ... "

"That's what you have. Yes. And it's not that hard, really. Every general down there wakes up in the morning thinking he could be El Presidente by the end of the day."

They sat in thought for a moment.

The Mayor said, "So they commission Rucker and his shop sets some plan into motion – insulated from the White House itself – and they fuck up and start to murder people to cover their tracks."

"Yes."

"Here's something for you. The jeweler's money-laundering scheme for the Colombians was being shielded by the FBI – and God knows who else."

"Really?" Hartman sat back and looked at the ceiling. The Mayor let him do the calculations. "Fascinating!"

"What do you have, Jerry?"

"Two weeks ago, our ambassador in Caracas gets called in by the Foreign Minister. He gets reamed out for a guerrilla attack on an air force base on the border with Colombia – Colombia, Freddy."

"The Colombians help Rucker put together a little army, they get a sweet payoff in New York, and some people get whacked here along the way."

Hartman nodded vigorously.

The Mayor sat back in his chair and stared absently at his desk.

"I think I'm going to pay a little visit to Tom Catapano," he said.

******

Ross told Tori he needed to see his mother and drove the Impala north through Westchester toward Green Haven Correctional Facility. He'd been there to interview cons before and needed only to flash his shield to have Alex Cordero brought to a quiet interview room.

"Do you know who I am?" he asked. Cordero was a skinny guy with sunken eyes and graying hair, the sort of person who might be mugged on a lonely subway car. He didn't look scared.

"You're the son."

"He had two sons. I'm the older one. I'm the cop."

They looked at each other without speaking.

"They say you're a model prisoner."

Cordero nodded vaguely. "This has been my life here. I tried my hardest to become a decent person. Twenty-three years. That's a long time." He looked out the door of the interview room, to avoid Ross' gaze. "Of course, it's not as long as forever."

Ross stared at him, wondering how this wisp of a man could have brought about so much heartache.

Finally, Ross said. "Show me the hand."

Cordero bit his lip and held up his right hand. "This one."

Ross tried to imagine the hand gripping a knife. If he hadn't had to check his gun, he could put a bullet in the hand, and maybe that would be enough.

"Let me tell you about my father," Ross said. "I was only nine when … when you killed him." Cordero winced, but nodded. "He had long hair, a beard – kind of a hippie. He was patient. Funny and fun. Always happy – at least around me. Used to take me fishing. He wasn't a tough guy. He didn't deserve to die like that. My mom didn't deserve to be a widow."

Cordero looked down at his lap.

"I deserve to die," he said finally. "If you're waiting outside the gate with a bullet for me, I'll understand."

The words changed something within Ross. "Go on," he said.

"I don't remember my father," Cordero said. "My mother never told me who it was. Maybe she didn't know. I got into trouble. Got sent to juvie a couple of times. Got into drugs. That became my life – stealing and drugs. And then crack came around, and I wasn't a human being anymore. I was a drug walking around on two legs." He looked out the door again and took a deep breath before he could continue. "I killed your father so I could get high for an hour. I've thought about that every night in here for 23 years. I know that doesn't bring your father back.

"I had to come here to become a whole person. To get away from the crack. I never went to school, but I read all the books they had in here and learned how to live life – regular, normal life. Not like wild animals in the jungle – the way I was." He studied his hand. The right hand.

"I think I'd like to step outside and breathe the free air and see the world without a fence in the way. If only for a minute or two. That would be nice. And then, if you want to kill me, that would be fair."

******

Tom Catapano settled onto a couch across from President James H. Morgan in the Oval Office.

"Sir, I wanted to bring you up to date on Lyle Rucker."

"Terribly sad business," the President said, biting his lip. "I'm devastated that the last time we met we had that ugly business. God, I hope that didn't figure into his suicide."

"I tend to doubt that, Mr. President. He had enormous legal problems. The SEC was all over his company."

"But that doesn't sound like Lyle. He was a tough sumbitch. I can't see him taking the easy way out."

"You never know, sir. We all react differently under pressure."

The President shook his head. "Well, anyway, I've

spoken to Debbie Rucker. She's holding up well. Of course, now she's in control of an international oil company."

"That takes some of the sting out."

"I'll say." The President grinned. "She told me – you'll love this, Tom – she told me that she understands her responsibility to support the party, as her husband had."

"Well what do you know?" Catapano flashed his trademark grin.

"Yes, it appears we wound up ahead of the game. Too bad Lyle had to wind up eating his gun."

"Yeah, well," Catapano said, "stuff happens."

"Indeed it does." The President smoothed his hair and crossed his arms. "What do they make of the North murder?"

"Drug gangs, probably. He was a shady character. All that time in Colombia. Some of those Agency operators forget which side they're on."

"Terrible. There's so much of that down that way. How did Lyle ever get mixed up with him?"

"I believe it was Reverend Nesmith."

"John Stanton Nesmith? The crackpot?"

Catapano grinned again. "The crackpot who bundles campaign donations like you wouldn't believe. He's *our* crackpot."

"Well then God bless his heart," said the President.

Catapano laughed.

"Tom," the President leaned across the table that separated them and spoke softly. "Who introduced North to Reverend Nesmith?"

Catapano grinned. "I did."

******

The office of Deputy Commissioner William Herron was undistinguished though spacious, as befitting his rank. Ross and Herron sat on his couch, beneath a photograph of a squad of cops in vintage uniforms and posed with bicycles. Herron followed Ross' gaze.

"They called them the Scorcher Squad," Herron said. "Teddy Roosevelt put them together. He put a bunch of cops on bikes so they could pull over speeding horse-drawn carriages."

"When he was police commissioner."

"Right, 1895. He knew you had to change with the times." Herron turned to face Ross. "You came through for us, Ross. Drew them all out and took it as far up the chain as we can go."

"You think it goes higher?"

"Yeah, I'm pretty sure. But unless we find them with a hot gun in their hand, that's for the mayor and the politicians to settle. We know there are people in government offices all over Washington who are playing outside the rules. When they come here, Ross, we'll call you."

"So I don't have to go back in the subway?"

"No," said Herron. "You're underground, but not in the subway. Your subway days are over."

"How far underground? Am I still in the department?"

"Oh sure. You still get your pension, and your badge. But I'm the only one you report to. It's not shoot first and ask questions later, but it's spy rules. We're not looking to hand over pretty cases to the district attorney. No headlines in the *Post*. No perp walks for the 11 o'clock news. Just beat the bad guys before they drop a body in the street."

Ross took it all in. He glanced at the Scorcher Squad. Teddy would have approved of this. He had just one question.

"What about Tori?"

Herron shrugged. "Better ask her."

******

Ross bounded up the four flights of stairs at the 28th Street apartment two at a time. He was surprised to find he wasn't too out of breath.

"I'm home, June," he shouted. "Wally? Beaver?" No answer. He finally found Tori in the bedroom. She was packing.

"What's this?" he asked. She met his eyes, unsmiling.

"What?" he tried again. "Are you angry? Did I do something?"

She shook her head and smoothed her hair. He embraced her and she hugged him tightly.

"Hey," he said gently. "You don't have to go." Then he added, "I don't have to stay."

She broke away. "Yes you do. You belong here. And I don't, Ross. It can't ... " She started over, fussing with her hair again. "We both knew this was a moment. A moment that would end. And here we are."

His mind spun but he couldn't retrieve a single reply – nothing that didn't sound utterly false. "We're a great team," he said at last, the words hanging like cold spaghetti on a wall. "And I love you."

"I know," she said. "Me too. I tried really hard not to, but," she turned to avoid looking at him, "we've got separate lives. I can't stay. And you know you can't leave."

"Yeah," he said sadly.

"I'm sorry," she said. "I didn't mean to —"

"I know. I thought you hated me."

She laughed, breaking the tension. "I thought you were such a jerk. And a horrible cop."

"But then you saw my brilliance. My powers of deduction."

"Yes." She smiled. "All of that. You're quite useful."

Ross took ahold of her hands and pulled her to him. "You're flying out tomorrow?"

"Yes. Very early flight from Kennedy."

"So let's go up on the roof."

"And eat out of cartons?"

"And eat out of cartons," he said. "And watch the lights go on in the city."

He kissed her, trying to record every sensation, to file away her scent, the way she felt in his arms.

"When the lights go on every night," he said, "that will be you."

Chapter 31

To meet inconspicuously, Mayor Silva invited Tom Catapano to the K Street office of the city's Washington lobbyist. The Mayor slipped into the building unnoticed; Catapano turned heads, but no one knew where he was going. It made perfect sense for him to be on K Street – Washington's premier operator in the heart of Beltway chicanery.

"Mr. Mayor, how nice to see you," said Catapano, smiling broadly. The Mayor smiled back tightly.

"Thanks for seeing me, Tom."

"Not at all, Freddy. Is there anything I can do for you while you're in D.C.?"

The Mayor exhaled and gazed out the window, south toward the World Bank building. Somewhere beyond it was the White House.

"I'm just going to come out with it, Tom." Catapano looked back quizzically. "You've got a black op spiraling out of control in my city and I don't like it."

Catapano flinched. "I see."

"Let me throw out some names for you, Tom. Yehuda Shapiro, Detective Ronald Margolis."

Catapano shook his head and held his palms up.

"Tony Bozzo, Michael McKenzie, Jason Hummel."

"I'm sorry, Mayor, I don't—"

"Eduardo Colon, Matt North, Lyle Rucker."

"Freddy what are you driving at?"

"What has the White House unleashed on my city?"

"What?"

"What mission was Lyle Rucker handed?"

For perhaps the first time in his adult life, Tom Catapano was expressionless.

"All but one of those people I've named are dead, Tom. And that's only because of a New York cop who happened to be right in the middle of an assassination attempt in Queens. In fucking Queens!" Silva felt his temper getting away from him. "Now you can give me some answers, or I can get a federal grand jury to get to the bottom of it."

Catapano exhaled as if he had been holding his breath. He crossed his arms and cleared his throat.

"It's a mean world out there, Mayor. We've got tyrants and psychopaths, terrorists, extremists – they're all out there trying to push us into a corner. Yes, we're doing secret ops to counter them. We wouldn't be doing our jobs if we didn't. Don't kid yourself."

"I'm not after you, Tom. I don't want to bring down the President. But I'm not going to sit by while thugs of any kind battle it out on the streets. My streets. I've got a pretty good idea of how all this came about. It would make a hell of a story. Not to mention a juicy case for the U.S. Attorney. The kind of case that vaults prosecutors into elected office."

"Freddy, think this through. If you were to—"

The Mayor held up his hand to cut him off.

"Let's just leave it at this: If one of your secret plans to save America spills blood in my streets, it's your ass."

Catapano began to speak, but stopped. He smiled. A Mona Lisa smile.

"Mr. Mayor, I understand completely. You have your job to do. I appreciate this talk, I really do."

The Mayor nodded. Catapano rose.

"As a matter of fact, Tom, there is something you can do. As you know, we've been trying to get federal funding for infrastructure and mass transit. The city is old and it's crumbling. If you could make that happen, Tom, then I think there's a good chance none of this gets leaked to *The Times*."

******

President Antonio Gallegos de la Paz was out of breath. He looked around the table at his military advisers gathered at Miraflores Palace, the seat of presidential power in Caracas. They appeared shellshocked after the President's 75-minute rant about U.S. aggression. General Manuel Abreau, the minister of defense, had lost track of the number of times Gallegos had invoked the name of Simon Bolivar, *El Libertador* – liberator of South America, or, at least, of much of the north.

"What do we do?" Gallegos roared. "What are our options?"

General Enrique Gomez, chief of the Army, spoke up timidly. "We can partner with the Cubans and attack Guantánamo," he offered.

The President's face, already red from his vigorous lecture, turned crimson. "And be attacked by the *Norte Americanos* and a coalition of their puppets? Have you no brain in that square head, Gomez! We want provocation, not war! They have nuclear weapons! We have jet planes."

"Presidente," General Abreau said, "I suggest a demonstration exercise, to show the *Norte Americanos* what we are capable of. We can overfly their territorial boundary. Send one of our ships into their Coast Guard waters. Some form of aggressive encroachment."

"Perhaps," offered General Armando Bustamante, chief of the Air Force, "it would be fitting to use the Sukhois."

Gallegos smiled. "Yes, the Sukhois." He got up and walked around the table. The generals nervously turned their heads as he paced behind them.

"We send the message that we are not to be trifled with," General Bustamante said. "If you poke the crocodile with a stick, he will come back to snap at you."

Gallegos nodded approvingly. He returned to his seat and tilted his head in thought, gazing absently at an ornate mirror. "What do you think, Bolivar?" he asked. Bolivar Dominguez, the President's senior adviser, was the only civilian in the room. Even the President was a military man, who frequently liked to wear his uniform, heavy with decorations.

"I think it's an excellent idea," Dominguez said. "It's provocative without being too aggressive. The *Norte Americanos* would have no traction at all in the United Nations. And to use the Sukhois is," he thought of the correct word, "a masterstroke. *This is what you get for your aggressions, President Morgan. Here are the very planes you tried to destroy, you imperialist devil. They know the way to Miami.*"

"Then it is agreed?" Gallegos asked. "We will overfly United States territory with a Sukhoi?"

"*Con permisso*, Your Excellency," said General Bustamante.

"Yes, General," said Gallegos.

"May I suggest a formation of at least three Sukhois. This will amplify the overflight and establish that it is not the result of a single pilot who had miscalculated."

Gallegos smiled widely. "Yes! *Excelente!*"

******

Catapano unlocked the door to his Georgetown townhouse replaying in his mind the conversation with Mayor Silva. He hadn't felt so flustered since he was a freshman at Stanford and he was caught unprepared in a political science class.

Catapano hadn't expected Silva to be so bold. He made a note to watch the young Mayor more carefully. He had the potential to go way beyond City Hall.

Though caught off guard, Catapano hadn't admitted a thing. He hadn't committed to the transit funding, either, though the stakes were far too high to fail to provide the money. The President would hit the ceiling over that, but Catapano knew how to reel in the big fish: Give him a lot of line and wait for him to decide it was his idea to get caught.

He would have to warn Bouton to be certain that whatever he launched did not erupt in New York. They were watching. He had heard about the cop up there who had snuffed all of Matt North's work. The poor jerk. North was actually just perfect for the job.

Catapano tried to imagine this cop as a New York version of James Bond. It was a tough picture to conjure.

Fortunately, Catapano had no engagements scheduled for the evening. The day's events had left him unsteady. He wanted only to open a good bottle of wine and lie in bed in front of the tube. What was America watching these days? Was anything mindlessly funny? Or just mindless?

He climbed the stairs and noticed a high-heeled shoe, and then another, in the hallway. They were deep blue. The housekeeper must have let someone in. Could Vanessa have had time to surprise him before filming began? Would she risk coming to his house? The shoes looked too large to be Vanessa's.

He found a blue dress, and a silk stocking. Lace panties. He entered the bedroom. Debbie Rucker was in his bed. Her blond hair fanned out around her.

"It's a new dress, Tom," she cooed. "Do you like it?"

The smile came back. "Very, *very* much," he said.

"Did I ever tell you, Tom, that I find power wildly, incredibly sexy?"

"Not in so many words, Debbie. Mind if I get in there with you and demonstrate just how powerful I am?" She smiled. "Well that's the idea, sugar."

Chapter 32

Tori settled into her window seat. A man in his mid-fifties shuffled up the aisle of the jetliner, stowed his carry-on in the overhead bin and took the middle seat. She looked up at him and he smiled. "I'll move over if we get lucky and no one sits on the aisle," he said. "But I wouldn't count on it. The airlines always fill all the seats these days."

Uh-oh, a talker, Tori thought. Men who found themselves seated beside Tori on a long, boring flight seemed to transform into nonstop conversationalists. She would usually go to sleep in self-defense. The flight to Denver was four and a half hours, long enough to go mad listening to the droning of a man unhinged by the presence of a tall, blond, blue-eyed, shapely woman.

"New Yorker or Coloradan?" he asked. He wore wire-rimmed glasses and chewed wintergreen gum.

"Um, going home to Denver," she said. He had nice green eyes and a relaxed manner about him. "How about you?"

"A little business, but I'm also visiting some friends in town. It's a nice break from New York."

"Yes, New York can be a little intense," she said. Not to mention Houston, she thought.

He smiled. "I often wonder why I live there." He reflected on his own words, then he turned back to Tori.

"How about you? What brought you to New York? Business or pleasure."

She thought of Ross. How he made her laugh. His lack of any pretense. His intelligence disguised behind a crude veneer. Did she love him? She was certain that working the job with him was exhilarating, that she craved him physically. Then why was she putting 1,600 miles between them?

"A little bit of both," she answered.

"Oh. What do you do?"

"I'm a consultant."

"Me, too! I do design. How about you?" A bedraggled woman settled into the aisle seat, fastened her seatbelt and shut her eyes. "Guess you're stuck with me now," he whispered to Tori as he tipped his head toward the aisle.

Tori smiled. "Consulting? I do work flow. It's better than it sounds. I get to travel a lot and meet interesting people." Like Mafiosos, contract killers and undercover cops.

He nodded and grew silent. She liked that. He hadn't even asked her name. He wasn't coming on strong like most of them.

"Did you get to see much of the city?" he asked at last.

Probably more than you ever have, dude, she thought.

"I did," she said. "I was working with a local guy and he," she bit her lip. "He showed me quite a bit. I have a lot of memories."

The pilot came on the PA system and stopped their conversation. Tori pulled out a paperback, but she couldn't focus on the words.

Once home, she'd throw down her bag and drive up to the mountains. Get out on the slopes. That would clear her head, and she could tuck Ross into a little drawer, where he would be safe to remember now and then.

******

Cordero's mother lived in a dreary walkup on Essex Street near Rivington – around the corner from where Doug Walton was stabbed to death so long ago. Alex Cordero, 19-year-old crackhead, was so addled that he violated the first rule of criminality: Don't shit where you eat.

Ross had confirmed that Cordero had walked through the gates and met his mother and a Yellow Cab driver. He'd breathed the free air and then some, and was back living in the neighborhood of his lost youth. Ross glanced at the intercom buttons: "4B Cordero." He pressed "5A Rifkin."

"Yes," said an ancient voice.

"UPS. Delivery for Rifkin."

"Is that the chondroitin? I ordered that two months ago."

"I have a package, sir," said Ross. "I don't know the contents." The door buzzed.

He climbed four flights of narrow stairs and stood before a battered door. An elderly woman answered the door at 4B. He guessed this was Cordero's mother, but he wasn't sure what to call her.

"Ma'am, I need to see Alex. I'm a friend."

She looked at Ross suspiciously past the chain that kept the door from opening more than a crack. "Alex don't know you." Those door chains were one of the biggest jokes in New York: a five-year-old could dislodge the four tiny screws that secured most of them with a modest kick.

"Yes, he does. Is he home? Tell him it's Ross."

"Why are all you people coming around? Leave my boy alone." She slammed the door. Ross could hear an assortment of bolts being turned.

He stood in the dim hallway uncertain what to do next. Above him, a door opened.

"Hey you," yelled an aged voice. "Where's my package?" Ross headed down the stairs. He was convinced Cordero was there; he was almost certain he'd heard soft footsteps approach the old woman as she spoke through the crack.

The weather had kicked into a higher gear of fall. Ross zipped his coat before stepping out to the street. Through the door, he saw a huge man walk south on Essex. About six foot seven and 375 pounds. Sally Beans.

Ross jumped back, his spine hitting a bank of mailboxes with a rattle. He looked through the door to see where Sally was going. The big man walked to the corner and got in a gray Acura with several other men.

Why are all you people coming around? Now Ross knew what Cordero's mother was talking about. *All you people.* They had come calling before Ross got there.

Ross called his mother.

"Ma."

"Hi Rossy. I was meaning to call you."

"Yeah, I know, Ma. He's out."

"Yeah," she said sadly.

"Ma, I gotta ask you something. It's important."

"OK."

"Tell me about the pledge."

"The what?"

"The pledge. The old man made a pledge after Dad got killed."

"Bacciagaloop?"

"Yeah."

"Rossy, I'd rather not —"

"This is important, Ma. Tell me."

He could imagine her mind spinning. The calculations she was making were about what might be harmful for Ross to know. She had never had much success in the world at large, but she was world class at the dual mother-father role.

"We were at the funeral home. The visiting. The old man came in. He wasn't so old then," she laughed faintly. "He was fat but not as …. Anyway, he looked at your father lying there and crossed himself and came over to me.

"Now, his family and mine go back to Sicily. That's a big thing with him. His father and my grandfather grew up together, inseparable. Like you and Sammy used to be. How is Sammy?"

"He's good, Ma. He always asks for you."

She took a moment to get back on track. "Uh, what was I saying."

"The old country."

"Yeah, so Bacciagaloop took an interest. He looked out for the neighborhood, you know, the people he liked, at least. And when that kid killed your father, he took that very personally. Very, very personally. He'd broken the law – his law. And he would pay if he ever got out.

"So, yeah, when he came over that day in the funeral home to pay his respects – his condolences and what-not – he leaned down and whispered, I'll make sure your kids are safe, and if that rat bastard ever gets out and comes back here, I'll put him in the ground."

Ross said a hurried goodbye and took the steps upstairs to 4B two at a time. He knocked urgently. The door opened a crack behind the chain. Ross thrust his gun through the opening and shouted, "Back up!" The old woman screamed. Ross took a step back and walked into the kick just as Tori had taught him. The chain mounts flew out of the wall and the door burst open.

Ross ran through the tiny living room. A Spanish variety show was blaring on the television. With gun aimed in front of him he entered one of the bedrooms. Cordero was sitting on the bed. He looked calm.

"I just ask that you don't shoot me here in front of my mother. Let's go up to the roof."

Ross stared at the man who had taken his father from him. Slowly, he lowered the gun.

"I'm not here to kill you," he said.

"I don't understand."

Ross was certain Sally Beans and his minions were about to come strolling in through the door he'd kicked in for them.

"We don't have any time for discussions. You have to come with me. You stay here, and you're a dead man. There's a car full of mob hitmen out front and they're here for you. Come on, we got to move."

Cordero sat there, puzzled.

"If I wanted to kill you, you'd be dead by now. Right?" Cordero nodded. "So you got to trust me."

Cordero shouted reassurance to his wailing mother as they ran out of the apartment. They heard footsteps, heavy and fast, on the stairs below.

"Up to the roof," Cordero shouted. "We can go down a couple and then jump over and come out a building on Norfolk." They ran up the stairs. Ross heard Rifkin's door open, but the old man heard all the commotion in the stairs and thought better of asking again about his chondroitin.

They emerged into a howling wind on the roof.

"This way," said Cordero, and they bounded from building to building. Cordero stopped and pointed to an adjacent building. It was a story lower and separated by an airshaft. "We have to jump. I did this a million times as a kid. Be sure to clear the airshaft. Hit the roof and roll."

Two spry wiseguys emerged from the roof entrance of Cordero's building.

"Over there," one pointed. The other squeezed off three shots. Ross and Cordero dropped to the deck as the bullets whistled over them. Hulking Sally Beans appeared behind his gunmen. The three mobsters began to run at them.

Cordero backed up a few steps, took a running start and flew across the gap. He hit the roof and rolled.

Ross cursed softly. He imagined landing awkwardly and being paralyzed. Like Eddie Ferguson.

Living a wisp of a life in a chair.

Another gunshot brought him back to the roof, the wind, the wiseguys and the airshaft. He backed up and launched himself. He landed in a crouch and let momentum carry him end over end. They ran down the stairs and out onto Norfolk Street. They walked a great loop around Sally Beans' car and back to the Impala.

"I think we've lost them," Ross said.

"Why are they after me?" Cordero asked. "I don't understand."

Ross looked him in the eye. "Those guys don't do parole."

They got in the car and Ross pulled away quickly.

"I've got a place for you to go until I can get this squashed," Ross said. "Stay out of the neighborhood until I say it's safe."

Ross dialed Luis and arranged for the Colombians to keep Cordero out of sight until Ross had talked to the old man. They drove to Queens to meet Luis' men.

"These are pretty bad people," Ross explained to Cordero as they bumped north on the FDR Drive, "but they owe me."

"I'm used to pretty bad people," Cordero said.

"I guess you are," Ross said with a grin.

Traffic was light; who could figure? Ross looked west at a cluster of Manhattan buildings. He pictured the skyline at dusk, as the lights went on.

Cordero looked closely at Ross. "Why are you doing this?" he asked.

Ross looked back at him. Cordero looked gaunt and frail. "I'm not sure."

Epilogue

Sammy Napolitano wore a tasteful pinstriped blue suit. He would have looked like another Wall Street shark if not for the black shirt and black tie. He spotted Frank Breslin in a booth toward the back of the restaurant and slid in opposite him.

"Whatsa matter, Frank? You don't look too good."

"What's right? That's a shorter list," he said, smiling. Breslin couldn't afford to be a mope in his line of work, where the word *problem* usually meant someone had been arrested or murdered. Most often the latter.

"I'd just met this guy who looked promising," Breslin explained. "I was going to hook you up with him. From Texas. Asshole buddies with the Colombians. Had some billionaire behind him and he was into all sorts of shit."

"Wait," Sammy interrupted. "I know this guy. North?"

"That's the one. He got clipped in Texas."

"He was a fucking ant."

Breslin cocked his head. "Huh?"

Sammy scanned the tables for familiar faces. The veal was good here, but he felt like a Caesar salad, maybe some fish.

"I heard about this guy," Sammy said. "He had

some political shit going on in South America. Then he was whacking people in New York to cover his tracks. He was an ant. Life expectancy of zero."

"What the fuck is an ant?"

Sammy gave him a look. "What happens to an ant when the lions run through the jungle? The fucking lion doesn't even know the ant's there. *Squish, squash, bing, bam.* That's what happened to this guy. He had no fucking clue about the games being played above him. Thought he was the king of the fucking jungle crawling around in the dirt."

Breslin thought this over. "Yeah, I see. I had a feeling this guy was gonna step in front of a speeding bus. Acted like he had it all figured out." He took a long sip of his Jameson. "So who did the guy?"

"Who cares? Coulda been anybody. Everybody." The waiter brought Sammy a Cognac. "Doesn't matter now. Dead is dead."

"Yeah, I guess."

"People got all excited when the terrorists in the Middle East were whacking off heads. But so what? You take a pill or some fuck chops your head off with sword – same difference."

"Dead is dead," said Breslin.

"Dead is dead." Sammy sampled his drink, then took a real sip. "But it's not all bad news, Frankie."

"Oh yeah?" Breslin said, "Why's that?"

"Cause you never run out of fools for a fool's errand."

******

Dennis Bouton drove triumphantly through the gates of the Old Executive Office Building. He had just enough time to stop by his office to collect his messages and check with the Situation Room for mayhem around the world. Pirates had snatched another tanker in the Gulf of Aden, but no one gave a shit as long as they kept away from U.S.-flagged ships. Nothing needed his immediate attention.

He hustled down the corridor to the office of his boss, Andrea Hopkins, the national security adviser to the President. Bouton believed she lived in that office. He couldn't recall ever seeing it vacant unless she was traveling. It was not uncommon for her to have spent the night on the couch.

"So what do we have?" she asked when they were seated at her conference table.

"Gallegos."

"Good. Good. We got a hold of some captured documents that establish that the Venezuelans are supporting FARC, who most of the Western nations consider to be a terrorist organization. The Man went nuts. Even cited the Monroe Doctrine. I had to remind him that Monroe was about threats from *outside* the hemisphere."

Bouton made an exasperated expression.

"He gets carried away."

Bouton noticed three pairs of shoes lined up behind her desk. "I've got more Colombians signed on," he said. "They're wired into street gangs in Caracas."

"I see."

"I've been in New York for discussions. They're on board."

"Who carries the water?"

"A shipyard owner in Jacksonville name of Mirtle. Rafael in Miami recommends him highly."

"Rafael does good work,"

"Yes, he does."

"And he's got a fabulous house."

"He certainly does. He offered it for a long weekend."

"You should go."

"I wish I could. Way too busy."

"Does Catapano know him? This Mirtle?"

"Of course. Tom says he's good people. And

better yet, Mirtle's got a fixer who knows his way around Maracaibo. He did the trouble-shooting for an oil company before Gallegos threw them out. An older guy – not a Boy Scout like—"

"Good," Hopkins said, ignoring the reference to the late Matt North. "You've got the green light. Just go slowly and don't miss. The stakes are high."

Bouton stepped out of the office. His adrenaline was surging. Back in action. Where to start first? He could wrestle with the details on the flight to New York.

ACKNOWLEDGMENTS

A deep bow and appreciation to my parents, Ruth Serviss and Marvin Serviss, who brought me into a world of books and newspapers and learning and travel and set me on this path of words and discovery. Thanks to Stan Wald, for encouraging me to finish the job when I'd lost my way, and to Barry DiSimone for his invaluable aviation expertise. Thanks to Jake Rome for a spectacular cover photograph and to John de Dios for throwing together an arresting book cover. Much thanks to my wonderful children, Emily Serviss and Ben Serviss, who gave me important feedback on the manuscript and who inspire me on a daily basis. You guys are the best. And most of all, thanks to Naomi Serviss, my partner in every adventure. Forever and a day.

Lew Serviss
New York City
2013

ABOUT THE AUTHOR

Born in Philadelphia, Lew Serviss is a longtime New Yorker who worked at newspapers in Buffalo, N.Y., Trenton, N.J., and Florida before joining New York Newsday.

He is now an editor at The New York Times and a contributor to the Committee to Protect Journalists.

Serviss lives in Upper Manhattan with his wife, the writer Naomi Serviss.

Made in the USA
San Bernardino, CA
11 May 2013